AN ACCIDENTAL
CHRIST

ABOUT THE AUTHOR

Lon Milo DuQuette (Costa Mesa, CA) is a preeminent esoteric scholar and the author of sixteen critically acclaimed books on magick and the occult, including *Enochian Vision Magick* and *The Chicken Qabalah of Rabbi Lamed Ben Clifford*.

AN ACCIDENTAL
CHRIST

THE STORY OF *Jesus*

(AS TOLD BY HIS UNCLE)

LON MILO DUQUETTE

Llewellyn Publications • Woodbury, Minnesota

FIRST EDITION, UPDATED AND REVISED
First Printing, 2023

FIRST EDITION, Thelema Aura, 2007

Cover art: Head of Christ, MET Gallery, Purchase, The Morris and Alma
    Schapiro Fund Gift, and Bequest of George D. Pratt, by exchange, 2014
Cover design by Shannon McKuhen
Interior maps by the Llewellyn Art Department

Llewellyn Publications is a registered trademark of Llewellyn Worldwide Ltd.

Library of Congress Cataloging-in-Publication Data (Pending)
ISBN: 978-0-7387-7351-3

Llewellyn Worldwide Ltd. does not participate in, endorse, or have any authority or responsibility concerning private business transactions between our authors and the public.
    All mail addressed to the author is forwarded but the publisher cannot, unless specifically instructed by the author, give out an address or phone number.
    Any internet references contained in this work are current at publication time, but the publisher cannot guarantee that a specific location will continue to be maintained. Please refer to the publisher's website for links to authors' websites and other sources.

Llewellyn Publications
A Division of Llewellyn Worldwide Ltd.
2143 Wooddale Drive
Woodbury, MN 55125-2989
www.llewellyn.com

Printed in the United States of America

OTHER BOOKS BY LON MILO DUQUETTE

*Low Magick: It's All In Your Head ... You Just Have No
Idea How Big Your Head Is*

Angels, Demons & Gods of the New Millennium

The Chicken Qabalah of Rabbi Lamed Ben Clifford

My Life with the Spirits

The Magick of Aleister Crowley

Tarot of Ceremonial Magick

Enochian Vision Magick

Then Pilate had Jesus scourged. And the soldiers wove a crown of thorns and placed it on his head, and they covered him with purple robes; And they said, Peace be to you, O King of the Jews! and they struck him on his cheeks. Pilate again went outside and said to them, Behold, I bring him outside to you, so that you may know that I find not even one cause against him. So Jesus went outside, wearing the crown of thorns and the purple robes. And Pilate said to them, Behold the man![1]

—John 19:1–5

---

1. All scriptural epigraphs are drawn from *The Holy Bible from the Ancient Eastern Text: George M. Lamsa's Translations from the Aramaic of the Peshitta*, translated by George M. Lamsa (San Francisco, CA: Harper San Francisco, 1985).

This work is dedicated to St. Constance of the Well
(Her Grace, Bishop Tau Justesse of *Ecclesia Gnostica Catholica*).

CONTENTS

AUTHOR'S DISCLAIMER

An Accidental Christ is a novel, a work of fiction. While the names of certain characters mentioned in the introductory material are those of actual historic figures, and while certain episodes outlined in the narrative describe bona fide historic events, the author is *not* suggesting (nor should the reader assume) the individuals spoke or behaved as depicted in the book.

NOTE ON BIBLICAL QUOTES

All scriptural epigraphs are drawn from *The Holy Bible from the Ancient Eastern Text: George M. Lamsa's Translations from the Aramaic of the Peshitta*, translated by George M. Lamsa (San Francisco, CA: Harper San Francisco, 1985).

PREFACE TO THE 2007
INTRODUCTORY EDITION[2]

Today a growing number of people are examining what is known and what is not known about the man who was called the Christ. For the better part of two thousand years, the only "historic" documents recognized by the great institutions of Christendom were the Gospels themselves. These texts offer to the intelligent mind more questions than answers. They abound with contradictions, inconsistencies, omissions, and errors in geography. So many and so serious are the irregularities in the Gospels that only those individuals who are prepared to sacrifice their better judgment on the altar of blind faith can still in good conscience embrace them as viable history.

What might have really happened to give rise to the myth of Jesus Christ? Modern scholarship, aided by the discoveries of the so-called *Gnostic Gospels* and the Dead Sea Scrolls, has provided us with a much clearer picture of the historic milieu of first-century Palestine: the politics, the cults, the Temple establishment, the movements, and most importantly, the activities of a sect or sects of highborn Jews who for generations awaited a "hybrid child": a child whose unique pedigree would make him the unquestioned heir to the mythological throne of David—King of the Jews.

I think it safe to predict that fundamentalist Christians will find *Accidental Christ* offensive and blasphemous. I did not, however,

---

2. Originally titled *Accidental Christ*. Privately printed limited edition.

write it in order to offend anyone. I assure you that, had it been my goal merely to be offensive, I could have done a much better job of it than *Accidental Christ* (and probably would have had a lot more fun doing it).

Simply put, *Accidental Christ* is a novel. It was written to entertain, amuse, and possibly stimulate open-minded individuals of all walks of life. Moreover, it was written to broaden the reader's spiritual worldview by introducing into the story many provocative bits of information that have come to light in the last fifty years—tiny bits, like the names of Jesus's relatives, and huge bits, like the nature of baptism or the fallacy of the story of the Egyptian captivity—bits that bring into serious question the historical veracity of many parts of both the Old and New Testaments.

After reading this little book, I encourage the reader to reread Matthew, Mark, Luke, and John and consider the possibility that many of the incidents described in those texts could have unfolded in a similar if not identical way to that which I have outlined in *Accidental Christ*. Some of my interpretations are necessarily speculative, and if I have taken the liberty of having some fun with them (e.g., the story of Jesus turning water into wine), it is partly to remind the reader that my text is no more an absolute "truth" to be accepted at face value than are the more famous tales upon which it is based. I want readers to remember that any great story is a mixture of fact and fiction, and this is certainly just as true of the "greatest story ever told."

Wherever possible, I have drawn my dialogue directly from the biblical texts. Please pay especial attention to book four, chapter 2, where Jesus has an encounter with the woman at the well. The dialogue between Jesus and the woman was taken directly from John, chapter 4.

For those who are interested in such things, the Gospel citations that begin each chapter are taken from *The Holy Bible from the*

Ancient Eastern Text: George M. Lamsa's Translations from the Aramaic of the Peshitta, translated by George M. Lamsa (San Francisco, CA: Harper San Francisco, 1985).

Unlike some contemporary scholars, I share Dr. Lamsa's opinion that the scriptures were not originally written in Greek but in Aramaic—the language of Jesus—and then transcribed, sometimes inaccurately, into Greek equivalents. The "Lamsa Bible," as it has come to be known, is based on ancient Aramaic texts (known collectively as the Peshitta text) that, to my mind at least, ring much truer in places than the Greek-based versions we have come to know. While I will always have a special fondness for the language and cadences of the King James Version that I grew up with, my determination to be as faithful as possible to the original text has made the Lamsa translation my Bible of choice.

Thank you for your interest. I hope you enjoy reading it as much as I have enjoyed bringing it to you.

Lon Milo DuQuette
Costa Mesa, California, 2006

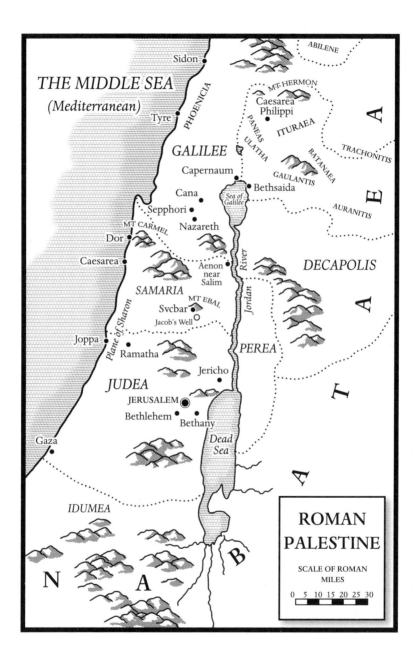

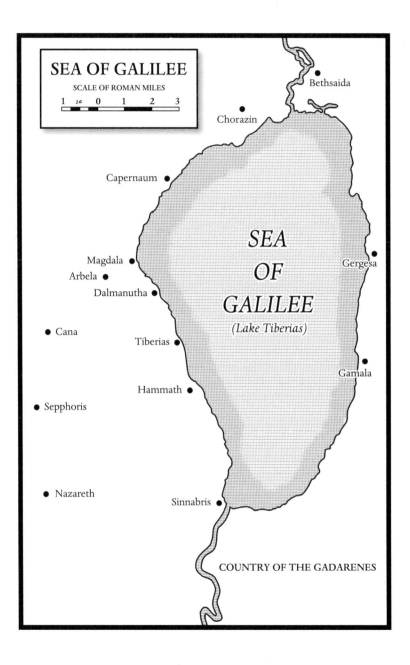

SEA OF GALILEE

SCALE OF ROMAN MILES

1   *1a*   **0**   1   2   3

Bethsaida

Chorazin

Capernaum

SEA

Magdala

OF

Gergesa

Arbela

Dalmanutha

GALILEE

(Lake Tiberias)

Cana

Tiberias

Gamala

Hammath

Sepphoris

Nazareth

Sinnabris

COUNTRY OF THE GADARENES

INTRODUCTION TO THE 2023 UPDATED AND REVISED EDITION[3]

Regarding the Clopasarian Manuscripts:
Background History and Provenance of Source Materials

MOUNT CARMEL SCROLLS

In 1949, two Bedouin shepherd boys seeking shelter at the foot of Mount Carmel (in what is today northern Israel) discovered a common clay amphora partially buried under a rough outcropping. The mouth of the vessel was sealed with beeswax and wrapped tightly with goatskin straps. After breaking the seal, they found within three parchment scrolls of obvious antiquity. They attempted to unravel the largest of the three, only to discover the fragility of the document prevented further inspection. Hoping their discovery might be of some value, they carried the amphora and its contents to Joppa and showed them to Abbud Ibrahim, a local dealer of antiquities.

Ibrahim examined the broken fragment from the largest of the scrolls and recognized the writing to be a form of archaic Graeco-Aramaic. It was penned in a style commonly used in formal documents of first-century Judaea. Paying the boys the equivalent of

---

3. *An Accidental Christ*, the novel, begins here.

sixteen dollars, he took possession of the amphora and scrolls and brought them to Dr. Constantine Zurayk of Damascus University, who immediately recognized the potential importance of the material.

Zurayk arranged for the scrolls to be safely unrolled, deciphered, and transcribed by a visiting team of archeologists from the University of Copenhagen, who examined and tested them thoroughly. It was soon determined that all three scrolls were indeed genuine first-century documents. More importantly, it was clear to Dr. Zurayk and his team that the material was of significant historic importance, as portions of it appeared to have been personally authored, dictated, or commissioned by an influential and well-known first-century Jewish nobleman, Clopas Ben Heli. Clopas was the half-brother of Joseph Ben Heli, father of the martyred first-century teacher and holy man, Jesus Ben Joseph of Nazareth.

While it is immediately obvious the bulk of the scrolls' narrative is not written in the first-person voice of Jesus's uncle Clopas, researchers are in agreement that the sections bearing the titles "Prologue of Clopas" and "Epilogue of Clopas" were indeed personally dictated by Clopas Ben Heli. The remaining material, while obviously written in the third-person narrative voice, nevertheless displays evidence of Ben Heli's supervisorial guidance and was clearly constructed upon his personal descriptions and narratives.

The importance of the Clopasarian material cannot be overestimated. Unlike the pseudepigraphic New Testament Gospels, which were written many years after the death of the holy man and teacher, the Mount Carmel scrolls represent a contemporaneous, firsthand, eyewitness narrative of events in the life of Jesus, written by a blood relative of the man himself. Moreover, the scrolls serve to cast further historic light on the circumstances surrounding the attempted overthrow of the puppet regime of the king Herod Antipas under the Roman administration of Pontius Pilate, the fifth prefect of Judaea.

This coup (had it succeeded) would have elevated Jesus Ben Joseph to the mythical Davidian throne of a united Israel-Judaea—literally establishing him as the hereditary "King of the Jews."

To the Christian world, the Clopas narrative offers a strange and unsettling version of the "greatest story ever told"—a story that Western civilization comfortably thought it already knew. For over two thousand years, Christendom's interpretations of the New Testament and its Gospel narratives have successfully crystalized in the popular imagination a familiar backstory to the miracle-laden wonder-tale of Jesus Christ. Unquestioned acceptance of the popular Gospel storyline as representing empirical history has bent the arc of religious and geo-political realities of Western civilization for over two thousand years. It should surprise no one that modern Christians, Muslims, and Jews in particular would be reluctant to entertain the real possibility that so many cherished religious and political traditions (especially those upon which the European divine right of kings was based) could have been so fundamentally misunderstood for so many centuries.

CLOPASARIAN CODICES

Needless to say, until 1949, when the Mount Carmel scrolls were unearthed, the Clopas narrative was not a subject of discussion or scholarly debate. Then, within two short years of the shepherd boys' find, three additional Clopasarian documents were discovered and brought to the attention of the public.

THE VATICAN CODEX (*CONFESSIO CLOPAS*)

The first (and most *incomplete*) fragment was brought to light in Rome exactly *two weeks* after the discovery of the Mount Carmel scrolls was made public. At a hastily called press conference at the Holy See Press Office, Dr. Bartolomeo Nogara, director of the Vatican Museums, announced the "chance discovery" of a small pamphlet-sized manuscript bearing the catalogue title *Confessio*

Clopas. Written in Latin on four sheets of sewn Italian vellum, the document appeared to have been carelessly misfiled in a twelfth-century portfolio casket of illuminated manuscripts on herbalism.

Tests on the ink, vellum, and molds conducted by teams from both the Vatican Museums and the University of Milan both confirmed the material composition of the *Confessio* to be of Maltese origin and copied no earlier than the twelfth century CE (over a thousand years later than the Mount Carmel scrolls). Interesting as the find was to scholars, it offered no new textual material whatsoever and represented merely two snippets from the opening sections of the Mount Carmel scrolls: the "Prologue of Clopas" and the five verses of the genealogical poem "The Song of the Vine."[4]

---

4. Abraham, Isaac, Jacob, and Judah;
   Perez and Herzon, Aram, Aminadab;
   Nahshon and Salmon, Boaz and Obed;
   The Father of Jesse, Sire of Great David.

   Nathan, Mattha, Mani and Melea;
   Eliakim, Jonam, Joseph and Judah;
   Simon, Levi, Mattiha and Joram;
   Eliezer, Jose, Er and Elmodad.

   Kosam, Addi, Melchi and Neri;
   Shelahiel, Zerubbabel, Rheasa and John;
   Judah, Joseph, Shemei and Mattath;
   Maath, Naggai, Hasli and Nahum.

   Amos, Matthat, Joseph and Jannai;
   Melchi, Levi, Matthat and Heli;
   The Sire of Wise Joseph, Scion of King David;
   The husband of Mary the Benjamite Maid.

   The branches are grafted to the root of the tree.
   Shunned Benjamin's womb bears King David's seed.
   The tribes are united, the Word is restored
   A King for all Israel, Messiah, and Lord.

Scholars are unanimous in the opinion (a rare event among scholars) that the Vatican "discovery" offers little more than general corroborating evidence of the empirical existence of Clopas Ben Heli and his historical role as a key player in the story of the life and career of Jesus.

One exasperated researcher even suggested the *Confessio* was nothing more than "a medieval attempt to reaffirm scriptural reference to Clopas without calling into question the doctrines of the twelfth-century Church of Rome."

THE EGYPTIAN SCROLLS

Nine months after the Vatican's announcement, a near-complete set of Clopasarian scrolls were discovered in Egypt by laborers excavating a first-century Therapeutae hospital on the shores of Lake Mareotis near Alexandria. The Egyptian scrolls were examined by researchers at Cairo University, who, after testing the ink, parchment, and traces of insect larvae, determined the provenance of the documents to be contemporaneous to (or within one hundred years of) the Mount Carmel scrolls. Variations in the hand of the calligraphers suggest it is unlikely they were written by the same individual scribe.

Most intriguingly to biblical scholars, the Egyptian scrolls did not include all the pages that appeared toward the end of the Mount Carmel scrolls, leaving researchers to conclude the Egyptian scrolls had been purposefully edited for reasons unknown. For several years, the Mount Carmel scrolls remained the document most relied upon by researchers.

THE TOULOUSEAN "DUPLICATE" (THE TRUE "ORIGINAL"?)

In the spring of 1952, workmen repairing a collapsed sewer in Toulouse, France found an intact Roman column together with its near-perfectly preserved Corinthian capital. When the capital was removed, the column was found to be hollow. It contained a copper cylinder within which was sealed the fourth, and arguably the most complete, of the Clopasarian codices. Unlike the Vatican and Egyptian material, however, the Toulouse document appears to have been written at the same time by the same scribe in the same location and using identical materials as the Mount Carmel scrolls. Additionally, the Toulouse scrolls contained additional material appended to the very end of the text, making it even more complete than the Mount Carmel scrolls. The fact that such an "exact" duplicate to the Mount Carmel scrolls was found nearly three thousand miles from Israel is in itself a most intriguing mystery.

Even though the Mount Carmel scrolls were the first Clopasarian documents brought to modern light, researchers now generally agree that the so-called Toulousean "duplicate" is not a duplicate at all but in fact the *true* original and that it had been dictated by Clopas Ben Heli himself in France sometime between AD 25 to 50. Certainly, there are broad hints within the narrative itself that suggest this is likely the case.

This theory begs the question: "How did the Mount Carmel scrolls (which were penned contemporaneously with the Toulousean material) reach the Holy Land in the first place?" It has been suggested, but without hard evidence, that the two sets of original Clopasarian scrolls might have been part of the legendary "secret" or "treasure" of the Knights Templar. While it is true that Knights Templar ships sailed regularly between France and the Holy Land (and the Templars were for many years active in the Toulouse area), this remains a matter of complete conjecture and outside the purview of this book.

To summarize, the Toulousean "duplicate" is now considered the most complete document for research. Its narrative is essentially identical with that of the Mount Carmel scrolls. The fact that it includes even more textual material serves only to enhance the integrity of the Mount Carmel document rather than obfuscate it.

WHO WAS THE SCRIBE?

The identity of the initial scribe/author of the work is unknown. Scribes were often anonymous and charged with the simple task of copying the material from draft manuscripts or from dictation. In this case the scribe appears to be an intimate colleague in service to Clopas Ben Heli. Clopas tells us directly in the dictated prologue and epilogue that the scribe is very young and resides in exile with Clopas and his family "in this verdant land so far from the bloody dust of Judaea." Elsewhere in the narratives it is suggested that this "verdant land" is Gaul (or France).

In his epilogue, Clopas makes a veiled reference to "a murderous former agent of Rome—a man who never met Jesus—is calling himself 'apostle' and poisoning the minds of even the elect with his hallucinatory gospel of fear and self-loathing."

This is likely a reference to the former Roman-Jew assassin, Saul of Tarsus. Saul (who after a head injury and a personal revelation called himself the "Apostle" Paul) was locked in a violent post-crucifixion conflict with James (the brother of Jesus), who had remained in Jerusalem to lead the remnants of Jesus's followers and the young Christian "church." This conflict ended with the murder of James and the essential hijacking by Paul of the young Christian movement. Clopas would naturally have been outraged at this turn of events.[5] If the reference was to Paul, then it would suggest the date of the initial dictation of the Clopasarian scrolls was very early in the Christian era.

---

5. It should be remembered that the "Epilogue of Clopas" was not included in the Vatican's *Confessio Clopas*.

SCRIPTURAL EPIGRAPHS

The reader will notice that each chapter of this book is headed by a biblical epigraph. The editors confess that these epigraphs were inserted to enhance the design of this book and were not part of the text of any of the original Clopasarian scrolls or codices.

ACCOMMODATING THE VARIATIONS FOUND AMONG THE SCROLLS

The reader will notice a certain awkwardness in the formatting toward the end of the book. This is the result of the editors' efforts to accommodate the several textual variants that exist between source manuscripts. Please know that the editors have done their best to provide the reader with as seamless a narrative as possible while faithfully preserving the integrity of each variant. Still, the reader will be obliged to draw their own conclusions about several matters, which may not be made clear in any of the manuscripts.

Please know that everyone involved in the publication of *An Accidental Christ* honors and respects the worldviews and the spiritual sensitivities of the various religions and schools of thought whose doctrines might be challenged or otherwise affected by the Clopasarian documents. Mr. DuQuette and the editors have made every effort to present the narrative in such a way as to allow the individual reader to draw their own conclusions.

Lon Milo DuQuette
Sacramento, California
Easter Sunday 2022

PROLOGUE OF CLOPAS[6]

There are also a great many other things which Jesus did, which, if
they were written one by one, not even this world, I believe, could
contain the books that would be written.

—John 21:25

Let it first be said that I am not the author of this story. The burdens
of composition have been mercifully borne by a younger hand that
never touched the flesh of the man whom they now call the Christ.
Indeed, the scribe was a young boy when the events that he so imag-
inatively describes occurred. He never trod the sacred soil of Palestine, nor can he in his youth possibly understand the full gravity of
the theme. However, to his credit, he has been a good student and a
loyal friend throughout my years of exile. Realizing that my life now
draws near its end and that soon I shall be gathered to my fathers,
he has prevailed upon me to read his vision of the story—a tale I
have recounted to him a thousand times.

I wish I could say his narrative is flawless in every respect, but alas
I cannot. Please do not misunderstand me. His overall understanding of the essential facts is profoundly accurate. The details, however,

---

6. The "Prologue of Clopas," as it appears here, forms the beginning section of all
   four of the Clopasarian discoveries. It also represents nearly the entire content of
   the Vatican's *Confessio Clopas*.

abound with petty inaccuracies—so many, in fact, that I abandoned my intention to itemize them for correction. For the most part, they do but innocent injustice to a few dates and features of geography, which are completely irrelevant to the story as a whole. Such trivial matters serve only to irritate the sensibilities of a dying old man who, because he can see no future, feels he must jealously preserve the past. I hope the reader will forgive the author, as I have done, for his litany of minor errors, realizing that ultimately the underlying truth is not revealed in the details. As progenitor of the tale, I unreservedly affirm that he has remained throughout an unyielding servant of the truth.

I believe, however, that future generations of readers might appreciate, by way of introduction, a glimpse into the historic milieu of the story. I am an adept student of the past, and I know very well that those who conquer create history to conceal their crimes and justify their infamies. It is inevitable. Information that is today common knowledge will one day be torn from cultural memory so that history can be remolded to serve the expedience of entrenched power. It is for those future generations whose vision of my world may have become obscured by time or villainy that I offer the following brief comments.

I am Clopas. I am a Jew of the tribe of Judah and a member of a royal family whose bloodline is said to spring from the loins of Israel's legendary warrior-king, David. Whether or not this is true matters little. I can no more prove the past existence of David than I can that of father Abraham or Isaac or Jacob or Joseph or Moses or Saul. They live in scripture, and scripture makes them real to my people.

My grandfather became wealthy in the frankincense trade. His wealth bought him power and influence. My father, Heli, before I was born waged a bloodless struggle with Herod the Great for the throne of Israel. The political realities of the day dictated victory for Herod, but my father, as consolation, was awarded spiritual stewardship of the vast multitude of wealthy Jews living outside of Israel and Judaea, especially those thriving in Ephesus and the five provinces of Asia Minor. These Hellenized but pious Diasporic Jews paid a yearly tax to my father who, in turn, forwarded a portion of the funds to Herod the Great for his monumental building projects. In addition to collecting taxes from the Diaspora, Heli created new Jews by baptizing Gentiles who were attracted to the concept of a single deity. My family had been prosperous for generations, but Heli's uneasy partnership with Herod the Great created a fortune that rivaled that of the king himself.

My father's first wife was also of royal blood. She died giving birth to a son named Joseph. Father married again the following year, and three years later, I was born. My half-brother Joseph would, late in life, wed a highborn maid of the tribe of Benjamin. A male child born of this union represented the mystical grafting of the bloodlines of Israel's first two kings: Saul (of the tribe of Benjamin) and David (of the tribe of Judah). In the vineyard of Jewish royalty, the fruit of this union was the hereditary "King of the Jews," whom many would hail as "Messiah," "the anointed one," and whom the Greeks called "the Christ."

I am the poor boy's uncle.

BOOK ONE

LAMB OF GOD

CHAPTER ONE

Now there was a garden in the place where Jesus was crucified;
and in the garden a new tomb, in which no man was yet laid.

—*John 19:41*

"*I thirst.*"

*Lazar rushed to the large clay basin that rested upon the
ground to the left of the crosses and soaked the sponge in vinegar
and gall.*

"*Try to get him to take two or three swallows*," *whispered
Brother Apollonius as he handed Lazar a spiked reed.* "*It will
work very quickly on a man of his weight. He should be unconscious in only a few moments.*"

*These words did not comfort Lazar, who knew that death
by crucifixion resulted from suffocation. Once his master was
unconscious, he would be unable to push his body up and
away from the cross to breathe. If he was not removed quickly,
he would die. If he was taken down too soon, the mob would
suspect.*

*Lazar speared the dripping sponge upon the sharpened
stalk of hyssop and lifted it toward the bleeding lips.* "*Master,
drink.*"

3

Jesus opened his swollen eyes, then dropped his head to take the venom-soaked sponge between his teeth. He swallowed more than he imagined possible before coughing up the last mouthful. His mouth and gums immediately became numb, and the burning in his muscles disappeared. He lifted his head and reckoned it was an hour to sunset and the start of the Great Sabbath.

He squinted to see the crowd of onlookers. Earlier in the day, they watched him scourged by soldiers; now they gathered at the base of the hill to see him die. Pilate's men were holding them at a safe distance. "At least that was going as planned," he thought. Would the onlookers really believe he would die after only six hours on the cross? After all, it often takes a crucified man four or five days to die. Could they see that he was only secured to the beams by ropes, not nailed to the planks like the two poor condemned souls hanging on either side of him? Death would come to them when their legs were broken. His own death must be the public humiliation of a nation—the crucifixion of a dream. Jesus envied his companions.

It became impossible to keep his eyes open. Determined to master even the conditions of his unconsciousness, he began silently to recite his genealogy—the litany of his fathers—the mantra of his duty:[7]

Abraham, Isaac, Jacob, and Judah;
Perez and Herzon, Aram, Aminadab;
Nahshon and Salmon, Boaz and Obed;
The Father of Jesse, Sire of Great David.

---

7. Jesus's genealogy as it appears here is referred to as the "Song of the Vine." The poem appears in all four Clopasarian documents including the Vatican's *Confessio Clopas.*

He could not remember a time when these names did not dominate his life. As an infant, they were his lullaby...

Nathan, Mattha, Mani and Melea;
Eliakim, Jonam, Joseph and Judah;
Simon, Levi, Mattiha and Joram;
Eliezer, Jose, Er and Elmodad.

...as a child growing up in Egypt, they were the prelude to his daily lessons...

Kosam, Addi, Melchi and Neri;
Shelahiel, Zerubbabel, Rheasa and John;
Judah, Joseph, Shemei and Mattath;
Maath, Naggai, Hasli and Nahum.

...as a man, they embodied the hopes of his family, his people, his nation.

Amos, Matthat, Joseph and Jannai;
Melchi, Levi, Matthat and Heli;
The Sire of Wise Joseph, Scion of King David;
The husband of Mary the Benjamite Maid.

Wise Joseph. Jesus tried to picture the face of his father. It was difficult. He dimly remembered a tall, frail old man who each year visited him at the academy in Alexandria. He was honored and respected by the Egyptian class masters who seemed quite eager to follow his unique requests concerning his son's education...

———

Joseph Ben Heli, the father of Jesus, was a direct descendant of King David and one of the richest men in Judaea. His father, Heli, had been extremely influential during the reign of Herod the Great and was, next to King David himself, the family's most revered ancestor.

As Jesus grew older, it became increasingly clear to him that his mother's marriage to Joseph was a singularly important event in Jewish culture. Mary was a purebred Benjamite and nearly thirty years younger than Joseph. It was a curious union, in more ways than one.

Since the time of the Judges, the tribe of Benjamin had been cut off from the other tribes by a terrible curse. Ancient tradition held that the Benjamites triggered a bitter feud with the priestly tribe of Levi by refusing to turn over certain infidels suspected of assaulting a Levite and butchering his concubine. In retaliation, the Levites, in their capacity as the spiritual leaders of the chosen people, promptly cast an irrevocable curse upon the tribe of Benjamin, binding the remaining tribes to vow, "None of us shall give his daughter in marriage to a Benjamite."

In the ensuing battles, the tribe of Benjamin was nearly exterminated. When peace was finally restored, less than six hundred Benjamite men remained alive. The other tribes lamented the fact that one of their own should be so cut off and feared that an entire tribe might become extinct. Nevertheless, the curse upon that generation could not be undone. To remedy the predicament, and in the spirit of reconciliation, the priests of Levi agreed to allow the surviving Benjamite men to steal wives from among the daughters of Shiloh in Bethel. (The men of Shiloh, because of their cautious neutrality during the conflict, were obviously too unmanly to deserve mastership of their women.) In the years to follow, Benjamites remained relatively few in number, but they were to grow mighty in land, power, and influence, even presenting Israel with its first king, Saul.

This paradox sprang from the fact that the choicest real estate in all the Promised Land remained by tradition the birthright of the tribe of Benjamin, allotted to them by Joshua when the children of Israel first slaughtered the original inhabitants and occupied the land. The Holy City of Jerusalem was the crown of Benjamin's inheritance, and the great Temple of God was its jewel.

The blood union of the houses of David and Saul had long been the dream of the orthodox nationalists. Such a figurehead could be a royal symbol to heal the thousand festering wounds of regional and religious factionalism that crippled the region. Under the right circumstances, a son from this union could rightfully be held up as the hereditary "King of the Jews." Such a star could capture the imagination of the people, usurp the power of petty kings such as Herod, perhaps even lead a revolt against the Roman occupation, and ultimately rule a united Palestine from the mythical throne of David.

> The branches are grafted to the root of the tree.
> Shunned Benjamin's womb bears King David's seed.
> The tribes are united, the Word is restored
> A King for all Israel, Messiah, and Lord.[8]

On Jesus's eleventh birthday the headmaster of the Alexandrian academy called him into his chambers. A stranger was seated near the window, a thin and angular man robed in white linen.

"Jesus, I present Brother Theudas, the patriarch of the Egyptian order of the Therapeutae. During your stay with us, he has served as your father's agent. He brings exciting news—news concerning you, my boy. In a few days, you will be leaving us and returning home to Palestine. It saddens me to think we will be losing such a bright young man, but a great adventure lies before you. I am confident your years with us have well prepared you for what is to come."

---

8. So ends "The Song of the Vine."

"Master, what is this about? I have not completed my classes. Surely my father would prefer that I—"

Theudas stood up and gently pushed Jesus down into a chair.

"Sit down, my boy. Sit. Sit!" Theudas was obviously very nervous. He paced back and forth across the room, cracking his bony knuckles one by one. He cleared his throat several times before speaking. When he finally began, his words tumbled from his mouth so fast that Jesus had great difficulty following his thoughts. "Your father and I are... are *colleagues*. He has instructed me to tell you certain important things on the day that you turn eleven years of age. I would prefer you heard these things from him, but he has insisted... and as we are old friends... I... I hardly know where to begin... to begin. Do you know who Heli was?"

"My grandfather?"

"Heli, your father's father, was a *David*... by that... by that I mean he was a direct and unpolluted... *undiluted*... descendent of King David. For centuries it has been the dream of our order and the Essenes and, indeed, all throughout the world of Jews who piously worship the one God... the one God... whose Name may not be spoken..."

The poor man became so flustered, he stopped to take a deep breath and clear his voice.

"...been our dream to restore a David to the throne of a united kingdom and also... also to install the rightful family of Zadok permanently to the high priesthood. Heli, *your* grandfather, was the first blood David in centuries to nearly accomplish this sacred task. He challenged Herod the Great for the throne of Israel, but sadly, it was not meant to be. Herod convinced... some say convinced... others say... well, it does not matter... Herod convinced him to be temporarily satisfied with serving as patriarch of Ephesus and all those of the Diaspora living in the five provinces of Asia Minor."

Young Jesus could not follow anything this man was trying to say. He interrupted, "Master, please, patriarch of who in Ephesus? What is the Diaspora?"

"Jews, lad. Jews! The Diaspora are the Jews of the outside world. Oh, there are so many more Jews outside Palestine than within her ancestorial borders, and unlike the natives, the foreign Jews have great wealth. How do you think Herod the Great paid for all his monumental building projects? Not with local funds, I assure you. Herod's wealth came from the Diasporic Jews who dwell in Rome and Greece and Asia Minor, people who gladly share their wealth to feel secure in their identity as the chosen people. Heli was their leader in Asia Minor. He swelled their ranks, year after year, by converting thousands of Gentiles. If they were not born Jews, he made them Jews by baptizing them, then teaching them the Laws of Moses.

"He was really quite amazing...then he taxed them...well...collected from them yearly tithes...and each year he brought this treasure to Great Herod and brought the Essenes and the other cults into alliance with him. For a while it appeared that your grandfather Heli would...that he could...with the support of an aligned Zadokite high priest...the family of Zadok are pledged to the Davids...but the time was not right...no...sadly no...not right for Heli...then...not right for your father. Great Herod is of course now many years dead. His son, Antipas, is weak...a buffoon...he has completely lost the respect and goodwill of the local cults and the Diaspora...Heli's old alliances have crumbled...but now...Praise him! Now! A Zadok is at last high priest...The time *could* be right for the David...Your father, Joseph...a prince of Judah...your mother...a Benjamite princess...You...You! You see?"

Jesus sprang to his feet. "I do *not* see! Sir, you must forgive me. I do not understand a word you are saying." Jesus turned to the headmaster. "Master, what has all this to do with me? It is my birthday, and I wish to rejoin my friends. Perhaps my father can better explain these things to me when he—"

"You!" Theudas shouted. "You, my young man...are the David of your generation! More than that...Do you not see? For all intents and purposes...your blood makes you...the rightful...the lawful...*King of the Jews!*"

Jesus sat down. "This is absurd," he thought. King of the Jews? Feuding shepherds and merchants whose only talent seemed to be a historic predisposition for disenfranchisement? He certainly did not want to be king of anything, least of all the Jews. He was not ashamed of being a Jew, but in his mind, he was an Egyptian, a student—a very good student. He was going to be a physician. He loved Egypt, the grandeur of its past and the wonders of its arts and sciences. Contrasted with the colorful tradesmen and calm philosophers of Hellenized Alexandria, young Jesus considered the Israelites to be a culture of superstitious tribesmen who slavishly worshipped a violent and fickle desert demon who demanded to be fed an endless flood of animal blood.

Although he could make no sense of Theudas's words, the look on the old man's face, and that of his headmaster as well, told him that these men were quite serious. He knew that this would not be the last he would hear of this "royal bloodline" nonsense. For the first time in his life, he wished he were someone else.

Soon after Theudas's bungling revelation, Jesus was returned to the land of his birth. However, he would not go to Judaea, which was too politically charged to be safe, but to Nazareth in Galilee where his family had relocated.

Here he was introduced for the first time to his five siblings. He had three half-brothers from Joseph's first marriage: Simon, twenty-six, was married with a nine-year-old daughter, and Joses and Judas were twenty-one and eighteen, respectively. His siblings from his parents' current marriage were James, who was born two years after Jesus, and his only sister, Leah, born a year later.

They spoke only Aramaic, and their rough provincial manners contrasted sharply with Jesus's Egyptianesque elegance. None of his brothers made any effort to hide the resentment they felt toward Jesus. Eight-year-old Leah, on the other hand, worshipped him from the moment they met. The five weeks he stayed at home were spent mostly in her company, telling her of life in Egypt. On the eve of his departure for his new school, she came to his room with a gift of a fresh fig.

"Father says you are a king, but James says it is he who is king because Mother and Father were not properly married when you were born. Simon says it does not matter at all, and if we tell anyone, soldiers will kill us. Are you a king?"

"Certainly not," he assured her.

Jesus was uncomfortable during the few weeks he resided with his family in Nazareth. It felt like he was living with strangers. He had been quite content with his solitary and studious life back at the academy. Unlike most of his fellow students, he delighted in the monastic discipline and rigorous study schedule. He loved learning new things and thrived on intellectual stimulation and philosophical discussion. He was brilliantly clever and made a habit of challenging his class masters in debate (often about subjects he knew little or nothing about). It seemed he did it for no other purpose than to fluster and paralyze his prey with argumentation.

Jesus was relieved when his mother told him that he would soon be enrolled in another monastic school. First, however, he would be taken to the Temple in Jerusalem for the formalities of his coming of age. His cousin John would be there also. The boys were nearly the same age and had never met before. It would not be a happy encounter.

Jesus was curiously awed by the spectacle of the Temple edifice itself but was not at all impressed by either the intelligence or the character of some of the priests and ostentatiously attired officiants. Following the ceremony, on the steps of the Temple, Jesus was anxious to cross intellectual swords with two of the priests on points of Mosaic law. John, who was intimately familiar with Temple decorum, tried in vain to keep Jesus from provoking them to debate. A small crowd gathered to listen and seemed delighted and amused at the scene. It seemed the two priests were not particularly popular with people, and everyone enjoyed watching them being embarrassed by a youngster. Realizing the danger this was putting him and his cousin in, John grabbed Jesus by the ear and dragged him off the steps.

"Were we not children, we would be stoned for this insolence," he hissed. "Who do you think you are? I'll tell you who you are! You're an arrogant little bastard! Bastard! That's what you are!"

Jesus was terrified and embarrassed. It would be the last time he and John would meet for many years.

————

Three days after the return from Jerusalem, Jesus was enrolled as a medical student at the Essene monastery on Mount Carmel, but no longer would his studies be focused on philosophy, mathematics, and Greek. Besides medicine, his duty now would require of him the mastery of other subjects: Hebrew, Aramaic, and the writings of the Hebrew prophets. A king, he discovered, must fulfill the prophecies.

The Carmelite Essenes differed drastically from their austere brethren in the south and were known throughout Syria and Palestine to be the greatest healers on earth. Their most powerful weapon was the knowledge that the physical body and the mind were inseparable. "Heal the mind and the body will follow" was the first precept of Carmelite medicine. The most effective way to do this, especially when dealing with the common folk, was to personify the illness as a spirit or a demon. A skillful physician could tap the energy of the patient's own fear and superstition and turn that power upon itself to exorcise the malady.

Obviously, this technique could only be successful if the original diagnosis was accurate. This *discernment* phase of treatment required not only an exhaustive mastery of anatomy and medicine, but also the ability to see the *spirit illness* with *spirit vision*. The order's detractors called this diagnostic trance "mystical surgery." Two centuries of grateful patients called it "miraculous." The common folk held an almost supernatural respect for Carmelite healers. So strong was their faith that very often a person who was seriously ill began to recover the moment they saw the white linen robe of the physician.

As impressive as the order's healing reputation was, its worldly *raison d'être* was permanent restoration of the Davidic monarchy and the priesthood of Zadok. To this end, they, more than any other sect, were the custodians of the history and central mysteries of Judaism. They possessed a magnificent library of ancient texts and employed scores of talented and disciplined scribes.

Both the northern Carmelites and the Dead Sea Essenes were strict vegetarians and did not participate in the animal sacrifice that was the focus of Temple worship. For this reason, they both were viewed with suspicion by the Temple establishment in Jerusalem, from whom they had severed ties in the days of the Maccabees and who now considered Essene philosophy too esoteric—perhaps even heretical. The Carmelites' preoccupation with the actual historic foundations of Judaism was especially unsettling to the Levite priests, whose power was based more upon myths, fables, and tradition than empirical evidence. It was no secret that the Mount Carmel library housed original and very early copies of the books of the prophets. It was even rumored that they possessed early drafts of Deuteronomy and other manuscripts, handwritten by Ezra the Scribe, which called into serious question the historical veracity of a centralized Hebrew culture and identity prior to the Babylonian captivity.

Most Essenes and Egyptian Therapeutae were celibate or else observed a strict code of ritualized breeding. However, in the north, in the communities near Mount Carmel, marriage was not forbidden; indeed, it was encouraged. Contrary to vulgar tradition, which used the scriptural fable of Eve's temptation of Adam to demonize the female's spiritual status, the Carmelites revered women as the temple of God in human form, a sacred spiritual vessel worthy to embody the Shekinah, the presence of the living God on earth. Being thus blessed by nature, it was deemed unnecessary (indeed deleterious) for her to undergo the same manner of harsh disciplines and ordeals required of men to achieve exalted states of spiritual consciousness. Her visions, counsel, and fellowship were esteemed throughout the community.

The school on Mount Carmel was strictly a male institution. Members of the lower grades were completely ignorant of the secrets and central teachings of the higher degrees. Jesus's celebrity status was known only to the abbot of the monastery, and he was required to endure the same challenges and austerities required of any acolyte.

After a two-year probationary period, Jesus entered into the degree of Faithful with a full-body immersion ceremony. The next two degrees, Illuminate and Illuminated, took two and three years respectively, during which time he endured subtle tests of his loyalty and integrity. Finally, at the age of eighteen (seven years after entering the school), he was formally raised to the degree of Perfect Master in an elaborate three-day entombment ceremony whereby "a man is raised from death to life."

Nowhere else on earth was this ancient (and sometimes fatal) ceremony administered. Only those among the Illuminated who were in the best of health and who had mastered the most profound meditative trances were eligible. No one who successfully survived the great ordeal ever feared death again. Of them it was said, "He is twice born and does not dread life, for he knows there is no dread afterlife."

A few weeks after Jesus was raised to Perfect Master, he became the personal apprentice to Brother Apollonius, the master physician of the sect. For the next eleven years, he labored at his side and learned the skills of medicine, for it is written, "Surely he has borne our sorrows and carried our griefs."

————

"He has stopped breathing. We must remove him from the cross."

Jesus could hear the frantic voice of Lazar but found it impossible to open his eyes or react. "There is no reason to be alarmed," he thought. Feeling had now returned to his feet and legs, a delightful soothing coolness.

He stepped into the shallows of the river. It was a hot day, and golden sunbeams walked upon the water; the dust of his long journey was washed away by the caress of the slow-moving current as Jesus waded into the river Jordan and toward his mad cousin John.

CHAPTER TWO

In those days came John the Baptist; and he was preaching in the wilderness of Judaea, Saying, Repent, for the kingdom of heaven is near. For it was he of whom it was said by the prophet Isaiah, The voice which cries in the wilderness, Prepare the way of the Lord, and straighten his highways.

—Matthew 3:1–3

Jesus was afraid of John. They first met as boys shortly after Jesus returned from Egypt, but their lives had been entwined long before they were born. Both were hereditary hybrids, blood-stars of Jewish royalty. John's mother, Elizabeth, was also a Benjamite princess and the great-aunt of Mary, the mother of Jesus. John's father, Zechariah, was the Zadokite high priest of the Temple of Jerusalem, supreme ritualistic officer of all Judaism. The marriage of Zechariah and Elizabeth had been formally arranged in order to breed a "David." In the days and weeks after John was born, it was he who was secretly heralded as King of the Jews and Messiah, and the elders scrambled to plot how he was to be groomed for coronation after the revolt.

That all changed abruptly when it was learned that Joseph Ben Heli, a wealthy widower of the House of David, had agreed to espouse a hybrid Benjamite maid and that she was already with child. Joseph's blood ran closer to the primary Davidian root than did

Zechariah's, and if Mary's child was a boy, *his* royal star would blaze brighter than John's.

Contingency plans were made. If Joseph and Mary brought forth a son, the child would be groomed as a future king, and Zechariah's boy, John, would then serve as the Messiah's herald and fulfill a key prophecy of Isaiah.

John was too young to remember his brief taste of kingship, but the pain of his father's disappointment remained visibly etched upon his face until he died. Still, old Zechariah was proud of his contribution and the role his seed would play.

"You must be the voice which cries in the wilderness," the old man constantly reminded young John. "You will prepare the way of the Lord, and make straight his way."

When word of the "Messiah" plot reached the ears of King Herod, the elders quickly decided that it would be best for all concerned if Joseph and Mary secretly took Jesus and sought refuge among wealthy sympathizers in Egypt. While Jesus grew refined in the comfort of Egyptian boarding schools, young John remained in Jerusalem and steeped to manhood in a broth of bitter prophecy and Roman brutality. Unlike Jesus, John embraced his hereditary duty with a frightening passion. If he could not be a king, he must be a prophet, and to that end, at the age of sixteen, he left the boisterous Temple school, gave away his possessions, and walked into the Judaean wilderness. There, among the blistering stones, serpents, and scorpions, he took the vow of a Nazarite.

The Hebrew hero Samson had been a Nazarite, and even though his fate was an object lesson in what happens to backsliding Nazarites, he was nonetheless a revered icon of the sect. Each year, spiritually inclined Jewish men seeking religious renewal took the Nazarite vow for short periods of time—seventy or one hundred days. During these retreats they remained celibate and wandered alone in the wilderness or otherwise kept themselves apart from the community. They fasted and shunned wine and the eating of animal flesh. More often than not, they wallowed in a background meditation of bodily mortification, during which time they allowed their hair and beards to grow.

Occasionally an aspiring holy man would take the Nazarite vow for life and become a hermit. The Judaean wasteland was peppered with these mad and colorful characters. No longer answerable to any community or religious standards, their spiritual quests were entirely their own and inscrutable to the outside world. Most preferred to begin with a year or two of complete silence, wandering the desert eating only herbs, insects, and "manna" (the small hallucinogenic mushrooms that sprouted on the sand in the morning dew). Some dug holes in the sand and sat there for years in continual prayer. Others whipped themselves or had others do it. No holy man was truly justified until he had consigned to absolute insignificance all distractions of body and mind. Eventually, even "self" was abandoned in the crossing of the great mystical abyss, below which "division is the result of contradiction," and above which "contradiction is unity."

Few aspirants ever achieved this transcendent "smooth point"— this "singularity"—where "Countenance beholds Countenance." Of those who did, most could not survive the influx of light. Their minds shattered like clay vessels struck by lightning. The Temple steps were littered with these naked and babbling stillborn prophets. John had gawked at them as a child.

At the age of twenty-eight, the individual known as John was annihilated in the desert of Judaea—dust lost in dust. He became the "smooth point." What remained behind was a voice…a voice crying in the wilderness. What once was the sacred duty of John, son of Zechariah, had now become the unbending will of the Almighty— his personal agonies the wrath of God.

CHAPTER THREE

Now this John's clothes were made of camel's hair, and he had leather belts around his waist, and his food was locusts and wild honey. Then went out to him Jerusalem and all of Judea and the whole country around Jordan. And they were baptized by him in the river Jordan, as they confessed their sins.

—Matthew 3:4–6

Word of John's bizarre behavior reached Jesus in Caesarea where he was visiting as part of his yearly medical tour. He had just turned twenty-nine.

He hadn't seen John since that traumatic day in Jerusalem—the day of his coming of age, the day he argued with the Levites on the Temple steps, the day John upbraided him, called him an arrogant little "bastard."

Jesus sat quietly beneath a fig tree and listened to the chatter of the villagers.

"Have you heard of the Teacher of Righteousness? He is a great prophet. Another Elijah."

"He speaks for God. He has hundreds of disciples."

"He baptizes them in the Jordan, at Aenon near Salim, to purify them, like babies, so they may be made worthy…worthy to receive the king."

"A Messiah is coming, and John is his prophet."

"I believe John *is* the Messiah. He waits to see who will follow him before he reveals himself."

"Have you heard? He has appeared at the court of Antipas and rebuked him for taking his brother's wife to his bed. Only Messiah would be that fearless."

Jesus squirmed and shook his head. Throughout almost two decades of training and preparation, he had come to accept and finally embrace the complex and dangerous plans that had been so carefully laid for his Davidian mission. It was not a life he had chosen, but a life that had chosen him. Although riven with constant doubts as to his own ability to become what others expected of him, he could not ignore the enormous responsibility that rested on his shoulders, a responsibility that literally flowed in his veins—a responsibility to his father, his teachers, his elders, and to unseen generations who believed that, when the time came, a true son of David would fulfill the destiny of a people and nation. And so, over the years, his youthful reluctance gave way to a sense of mission.

He knew that his childhood nemesis had an important role to play in that mission, but John himself seemed unaware of it, or worse, was driven to pervert it. John had become a madman. The elders most certainly did not encourage him to begin this phase of the Plan. Did he know what he was doing? Was he trying to ruin everything?

"Not now, John!" Jesus whispered to himself. He wasn't ready for the great adventure to begin. He wasn't sure if he would ever be ready. He didn't know if he *wanted* to be ready. Now more than ever he wished his father were still alive. He must stop John. No, first he must talk to his uncle Clopas and the elders.

Jesus returned immediately to the monastery and informed the abbot he was departing.

"Master, please know that if it were my will, I would be content to end my days as a physician in service to our order."

The abbot received the news with a combination of sadness and great excitement.

"We knew this day would come. You of course must go now." The old man clapped his hands to summon his Illuminated valet. "Lazar! Our Brother Jesus will be leaving us. Instruct Brother Micaiah to prepare a bountiful purse for his journey."

Lazar turned to execute his master's orders, but before he reached the door, the abbot added, "And draw the Messiah and me a pitcher of that delicious Chalybon."

The young man was visibly startled by the abbot's apparent blasphemy, then, thinking he was being teased, let out a nervous giggle and disappeared down the hall.

This surprised Jesus as well. Carmelite Perfect Masters were not forbidden to drink wine; on the contrary, it was an indispensable ceremonial element of the daily communion supper. However, it was not a common practice to imbibe socially. The choice of Syrian Chalybon, the prized nectar of Persian kings, signaled this was a particularly auspicious moment.

Lazar returned carrying a tray containing two cups, a large pitcher of wine, a pitcher of water, and a small silver platter of freshly baked bread. Dismissing the boy, the abbot poured them each a full cup of the sweet ambrosia.

"The blood of both David and Saul is said to run through your veins. Some would believe it to be holy blood. Let them if they need to." He closed his eyes and raised the mouth of the cup to his nose and drew in a deep breath. His face radiated with ecstasy. Without a word, he lifted the vessel to his lips and took a small sip. He bathed his tongue for just a moment, then unceremoniously drained the entire cup. Jesus, not wishing to offend, did the same. It was gloriously delicious. It instantly took effect, and a glow of warm excitement seized his heart and solar plexus.

"'Seekers after smooth things.' That's what other Essenes call us," the abbot remarked. "Especially our chaste brothers and sisters living near the Dead Sea. Life is difficult enough without shunning modest pleasures. Do you not agree, my son?"

The abbot didn't wait for an answer; he stood up and refilled their cups. "I know some things that may help you."

In eighteen years, Jesus had never seen the abbot like this. He was candid, humorous, and animated. He spent the remainder of the afternoon revealing the names and locations of dozens of friends of the order who were supporters of the "Messiah movement," as he called it. These names he wrote in an alphanumeric cipher upon a small scroll. The list included prominent members of both sides of the family of Jesus, individuals from among the various cults including the Essenes, Nazarites, Therapeutae, Sadducees, and not surprisingly, leaders of the militant Zealators.

Then, lowering his voice, he whispered, "Even a member of the great Sanhedrin will help you. His name is *never written*, not even in cipher. He alone will reveal himself to you. All of them look for a king, and all of them for different reasons. Our Dead Sea brethren, living in their bizarre little replica of Jerusalem, dream of uniting the Diaspora and returning them home to witness the end of the world. Your family expects another David; the Zealators need a revolutionary warrior—a Judah Maccabee; the Sadducees look for the High Priest Zadok, and the Nazarites..." The old man ruffled his hair and rolled his eyes madly in mock derangement. "...the Nazarites will expect you to evoke a baptism of fire that will consume all that is not the perfect will of God."

The two laughed like bibbers in a tavern.

The abbot straightened his thinning hair and took another sip of wine. "Beware the Pharisees. They may quibble like passionless bookworms, but their infinite obsession with the splitting of spiritual hairs is just the kind of meaningless distraction Rome likes her vassals focusing on. They are powerful, and they will tolerate no thought that is not their own. They are particularly suspicious of Essenes."

By late afternoon, the two had nearly finished the entire pitcher of wine. The old man poured the last trickles into both cups, pretending to be scrupulously fair, then leaned back and fell silent.

"The vulgar will need a shepherd, for they go where they are pointed. They are children—innocent, cruel, and superstitious. They can be easily wooed with 'miracles' and stories that sound like they veil other stories. They are the most important element in the equation, my friend. They are also dangerously unstable."

"But I am no Judah Maccabee or wonder-worker," protested Jesus. "As far as capturing the hearts of the people, you know how retiring I am around outsiders. If I am not healing them, I avoid conversing with them."

"Already you are a master healer. Your powers of discernment are equaled only by those of Brother Apollonius. He will grieve deeply when he hears his most talented physician has left the community. Miracles, like healing, are in the minds of those who suffer. The people have been afflicted for generations, first by civil wars, then by Rome. They are ready to seize and swallow any medicine that is presented as such and will shout that they are healed. Their faith is intense enough to move mountains, but beware, their attention span is pathetically short. The same that wash your feet shall stone you. Your disciples will be idiots, and those that love you will be more dangerous than your enemies.

"But fear not, dear friend. 'A Perfect Master does not dread life, for he knows there is no dread afterlife.'" With that, the old abbot struggled to his feet, kissed Jesus, and gave him his blessing.

———

Ramtha was in northern Judaea, about sixty Roman miles due south of Mount Carmel. It was the home of Jesus's uncle Clopas who, since the death of Wise Joseph, was head of the family and custodian of the Plan. It was a pleasant enough journey, first by sea from Dor to Joppa, then about ten miles inland across the fertile Plain of Sharon. Everywhere he stopped, the people were abuzz with stories of John the Baptizer and the coming king. It was becoming increasingly clear that John was operating on his own timetable. He could never be a part of anything that resembled an organized plan. If he wasn't handled carefully, he could ruin everything.

Four days after leaving the monastery, he arrived at Ramtha and the home of the portly half-brother of Joseph. Like most of Jesus's relatives, Uncle Clopas was wealthy. His grandfather's fortune was made trading in frankincense. It was a point of pride that the fine olibanum that burned perpetually in the Temple of Jerusalem had been supplied by the family for four generations. Clopas increased the family's fortunes tenfold by building his own fleet of sailing vessels harbored at Joppa, and began trading lumber imported from Tyre and Sidon. Joseph, the father of Jesus, was the major investor and senior partner in this venture. In the early years, Joseph prospered so much by the sale of Lebanese cedar that he was called the "Great Carpenter" throughout Galilee and northern Judaea.

Of all of Jesus's relatives, Clopas was the most Hellenized. He loved all things Greek and was a classical scholar without equal among Jews. As a young man he traveled extensively, pursuing pleasures of the flesh in Corinth, knowledge of the heavens in Persia, and

wisdom of the soul in Greece. He even had been accepted as an initiate of the mysteries of Demeter and Persephone at the citadel of Ele-
usis. His great wealth and generosity to the Temple immunized him
from the wrath of orthodox critics at home.

"Jesus, my boy, my boy, my boy!" Clopas waddled into the courtyard to embrace his nephew. After a lengthy hug that included a score
of wet kisses, he released his prey. "You're so thin! Does the abbot
feed you nothing but wisdom on the mountain?"

Not waiting for an answer, he ushered Jesus to the portico and
called his wife and daughter. "Mary, Naomi, quickly! Come wash
the feet of the son of Wise Joseph." Before the women appeared,
he grabbed Jesus by the arm and pulled him close. "You have come
because of John, haven't you? Listen to me! He is quite mad, you
know. Quite mad, indeed. He has eschewed the elders. Won't listen
to any of us. He has become the darling of the Dead Sea Essenes. Oh
yes, he is just their type—a madman who thinks a penis is only for
pissing. Yes, we must make plans. There is no turning back now. Our
deliverance is at hand, my young Messiah."

CHAPTER FOUR

Thus says Cyrus king of Persia: The Lord God of heaven has given me all the kingdoms of the earth, and he has commanded me to build him a house in Jerusalem, which city is in Judah. Who is there among you of all his people? His God be with him, let him go up to Jerusalem, which is in Judah, and build the house to the Lord the God of Israel, he is the God who is in Jerusalem.

—Ezra 1:2–3

Jesus remained a little over six weeks at the home of Uncle Clopas, where he was assailed each day from dawn to midnight with the details of nearly three hundred years of scriptural mythology, empirical history, politics, and religion.

In the weeks that followed, Clopas introduced Jesus to scores of confederates and fellow travelers, all of whom treated him as if he were already anointed and crowned. Then, early one morning, he met a very different kind of conspirator, one who would forever change the way he would think of himself.

"Jesus, wake up!" It was still dark. The voice was that of his aunt Mary, who stood at his chamber door with an olive oil lamp. Jesus wiped dreams of Egypt from his eyes.

"We have a very important guest who wants to meet you. Dress quickly and meet your uncle in the study." She then turned and disappeared down the narrow hall, taking the light with her.

An important guest? At this time of night? Jesus grumbled to himself as he groped in the darkness for his robe. Once dressed, he drowsily stumbled down the darkened hallway, bouncing every few steps against one wall, then the other.

Nearing the study, he was startled to see two Temple soldiers standing in the doorway. Upon his approach, they stood shoulder to shoulder to bar his entry.

"Please! Let him pass." From behind them, Clopas tried to shout and whisper at the same time. The soldiers fell back into the study and cleared a path. Clopas stood in his nightshirt, his hair so disheveled he appeared a bit mad.

"Jesus, Jesus, dear boy, there is someone who would like to…I mean, there is someone I want *you* to meet." Clopas was uncharacteristically flustered. Jesus was now frightened fully awake.

The man sitting across the table from Clopas was dressed in costly riding clothes and smelled of a horse that had been ridden hard. He was large but not as plump as Clopas. His face was covered from the nose down with the chin flap of his turban.

"You look frightened." The masked face had a voice. "Were you not taught to be fearless? Of course you were. 'Such as we do not dread life, for we know there is no dread afterlife.'"

This allusion told Jesus he was in the presence of a fellow Perfect Master and the key conspirator of whom the abbot had spoken in whispers.

Clopas ventured to speak again. "My boy, may I introduce Joseph of Ramtha, the lord of our community and a senior counselor to the Sanhedrin in Jerusalem."

Joseph stood up and uncovered his face. He appeared to be in his mid-sixties, a full head shorter than Jesus. His face was a brownish gray, like lentil paste, and showed a scattering of darker spots that appear with age. His dark gray beard disappeared under the neck of his garment, and his eyebrows jutted sharply forward like awnings sheltering two sparkling black orbs. Jesus thought they looked like the eyes of a hawk.

Jesus opened his mouth to speak when, to the wonder of all in the room, Joseph of Ramtha dropped slowly to his knees, then fell completely prostrate on the floor before the feet of Jesus. "I am your servant, Jesus Ben Joseph Ben Heli, King of the Jews."

After a moment of confused hesitation, all others in the room did likewise, including Clopas, who had considerable difficulty getting up again. At first, Jesus thought he was being mocked. He felt uneasy and embarrassed and insisted that everyone get off the floor and take their seats.

Once settled, Joseph spoke quietly and with great deliberation. "Soon the sun will rise. When it does, I would like you to climb to the roof of this house. As far as you will be able to see in every direction is the province of my family and has been for generations. I am the wealthiest man in northern Judaea. For one hundred and seventy years, members of my family have served selflessly in all levels of commerce, religion, and politics. Do you want to know *how* we have kept our wealth and position throughout generations of civil strife and foreign occupation?"

"Because you have collaborated?" Jesus surprised himself with his audacious reply. No one said a word. Clopas stirred uncomfortably.

Joseph answered with an icy glower that caused Jesus to look away. "Yes, we collaborate." He stood up and walked to the window and stroked his eyes with both hands as if he was trying to rub images from his mind onto his lips. "Religion and government are two clan-destine lovers who must *never* commit to marry. Separately, they have the potential to enlighten our minds, comfort our hearts, sustain our bodies, and free our souls. But once they are bound to one another, they become a single entity...a devil...a self-devouring devil.

"Our scriptures would have us believe we are God's chosen. But the same scriptures describe us as a stiff-necked people. Our God teases us with covenants he will never honor because he is omniscient and knows in advance we are too human to realize his ideal. Still, he punishes us. He scourges us with many rods. He gives us land, then blesses our enemies who take the land from us. He delivers us into bondage, then permits us to return to become slaves within our very borders.

"Yes, Jesus Ben Joseph, you are correct. In order to survive, col-laboration has become for us an art form—an exercise of perverse worship. First, we collaborate with a God for whom punishment is a token of love; then, we collaborate with the very instruments of his wrath. We wallow in our woe. We are more self-indulgent in our suf-fering than the foaming-mouthed pain worshipers of Corinth who ejaculate only after torture."

"Forgive my insolence, Lord Joseph," Jesus said. "But are *we* not attempting to openly wed the clandestine lovers of government and religion? If we succeed, will we not be creating the great devil? If that is the case, I believe the king should fear most the madness of his own subjects."

Joseph turned and looked at Clopas, and then broke into a broad smile. "Wise indeed is the monarch who would spurn a kingdom of fools!"

Then everyone in the room except Jesus laughed as if they under-stood a subtle meaning in Joseph's statement.

"Yes," Joseph answered. "On the surface it will appear to the world that our Davidic kingdom is a theocracy. But for any kingdom to exist it must first *appear* to be *something*."

Joseph returned to his seat and drew it closer to Jesus. "You are a well-educated man. I have no doubt you are aware that the legendary kingdoms of David and Solomon, if they existed at all, bore little semblance to the fanciful scriptural accounts. We both know that much of what is commonly believed to have been the golden age of ancient Israel is fiction, a fantasy spun by the melancholy poets of the Babylonian captivity—a dream to bring hope to the diverse captives of that cruel era. When Great Cyrus conquered Babylon, he found it necessary to expeditiously rid himself of our ancestors and the other slaves Nebuchadnezzar had captured from foreign lands."

"After two generations, our forefathers had become too expensive to feed and too numerous to house," Uncle Clopas laughingly interjected.

Joseph did not acknowledge the interruption. "Darius, Cyrus's successor, feared cultural unrest if he were to attempt to assimilate this throng into Babylonian society, and he certainly didn't want to bring them to Persia. So he conspired with the holy man Nehemiah and the scribe Ezra to create a single identity for these poor souls. In order to give them a future, it was first necessary to create for them a past, so to explain the diversity of their languages, dialects, and customs, Ezra convinced them that each group sprang from one of twelve distinct *tribes* of mythical *Hebrews*."

Clopas interrupted again. "Thus was Moses drawn, not from the ancient imaginary bulrushes of the Nile but from the very real imaginations of good men who wished to free an assortment of people possessing no cultural memory whatsoever."

Joseph smiled warmly at Clopas. "Thank you, Clopas. Yes. Exactly. The children of the captivity eagerly accepted this vision, and with great fervor believed with all their hearts that they were the children of the mythical patriarchs. The scribe Ezra gathered scraps of local legends and myths that still echoed in the minds of the various 'tribes' and retold the stories as the Five Books of Moses. To further bolster the self-identity of the 'tribes,' King Darius freed them to return to their 'homeland'—an area that was ruled by no king and defended by no army. He gave them Palestine if they promised to immediately leave Babylon."

Uncle Clopas cleared his throat and stood up. It was obvious that he had rehearsed what he was about to say. He delivered his words with the accentuation of a schoolmaster. "There was indeed an exodus, my lords. But the exodus was from Babylon, *not* from Egypt. In a word, my lords, our magnificent religion and the nations of Israel and Judaea are children of a dream—the awkward consequence of expedient Persian politics."

Jesus knew what these men said was true. Of all the cults, the Carmelites had no delusions concerning the secret history of the faith.

The room remained silent for a moment, then Joseph of Ramtha spoke directly to Jesus. "However, *you*, my lord, are both real *and* fantasy. History and myth unite in your blood. You are not only a real king, but also king of a dream—the rightful heir to a kingdom prepared for you from the foundation of the world."

"But surely there have been others in the past who could have been put forth as king!" Jesus protested. "My grandfather Heli, or my father—"

"Ah! That is where you are wrong." Clopas came to life and jumped to his feet. "Your mother's blood holds the key. See here!" Carrying a lamp to the far wall of the kitchen, he revealed it to be festooned with five different variations of the family tree of Joseph, and no less than sixteen of Mary's.

"You are the true vine, my boy, and your father was the last master gardener. Your blood is the rarest fruit of our race. You are a star fixed in the heavens of our people! When news of your birth reached the Diaspora in Persia, they dispatched a party of astrologers to verify your lineage. Can you imagine how upset Great Herod became when the Magians came to *him* asking to see the child who was '*born* King of the Jews'? Herod knew then and there he had lost the support of the cults. What a slap in the old flatulent's face! Almost cost us all our lives too.

"But I digress. The scribe Ezra created family trees for David and Solomon in abundance. These here prove you to be the preeminent scion of *both houses*, without question. Follow the streams of blood from David and Saul. They have nearly touched only three times in generations past, most recently with your great-grandfather Matthat, then here at your grandfather Heli, and most recently with your cousin John." Clopas paused and mumbled something under his breath. Then he continued, "But! But, because of the unique and fortunate grafting of both *your* parents' sires and dames, the streams of Israel's first two legendary kings actually merge in *you*! They merge! Don't you see? Listen to me. 'Shunned Benjamin's womb bears King David's seed.' It is as if King Saul wedded King David and gave birth to *you*!"

Clopas almost wriggled with excitement and pointed back and forth at the trees.

"These trees were reviewed and approved by the Magians when you were born. See here their seals. The charts over here trace your ancestry back from Solomon and David to Abraham—to Adam! These other trees were cast by the Temple genealogists who calculated your descent from Adam—Adam, Seth, Enosh, Cainan, Mahalalael, Jared, Enoch, Methuselah, Lamech, Noah, Shem, Arphazar, Cainan, Shalah, Eber, Peleg, Arau, Serug, Nahor, Terah, Abraham, and on to you! The High Priest Zechariah himself reviewed these charts over here. See here his seal.

"No, no, my young friend. Listen to me! There has only been one like you...only *one*."

"But what about my younger brother, James?" Jesus asked. "Do not the same streams merge in him as well?"

"James is but the *second* fruit of your parents' loins," snapped Clopas.

"Ah! But I understand there is controversy surrounding the circumstances of my birth. It is true, is it not, that I was conceived prematurely during the betrothal period prior to the formal wedding? Even my cousin John calls me a bastard."

"Yes!" Joseph interrupted sharply. He drew in his breath and held it as if he were reluctant to speak. "Know this well. Your conception and birth conformed lawfully to the marriage protocols of the two sects to which your mother and father belonged. But yes. It is true. According to the complex and archaic breeding protocols of other cults, your conception occurred in the period after the *betrothal* but before the *wedding* was sealed. In the eyes of these cults, your mother was legally a *virgin*, and you are a *bastard* who should have been exposed at birth."

"Nonsense!" Clopas scoffed.

Joseph of Ramtha raised his voice. "I will be frank with all of you. It is true. If the coup were to take place today, the leaders of several of these cults would hasten to recognize your brother James but not you. But the coup is *not* taking place today and will take at least *three years* before we are ready to strike. I assure you, by then these superstitious old pharaohs will be unable to voice their objections. It is *Jesus*, not James, who has been educated, initiated, and groomed for kingship. It is through the veins of *Jesus* that the mythical blood of David and Saul first flowed in our generation."

"But my blood is no holier than yours or the leper outside the city gate," Jesus said almost under his breath.

"That is true," said Joseph. "Nevertheless, it is a vitriolic acid with the power to dissolve the throne of the Herods. If we can keep the various factions and cults off-balance until your ascension, they will all race to be first to receive your royal blessing. Unlike the Herodians who have kept their puppet power by fomenting feuds, you will wield the full force of a united theocracy. Rome will be relieved to negotiate a more reasonable accord…and we will make it very clear to Rome that you *will* be a *reasonable* king."

The tone of Joseph's voice changed with these words. He leaned over and placed his hand on Jesus's hand and pressed down for emphasis.

"I know for a fact that Rome is weary of wasting her legions occupying this land of dust and scorpions. She dreams nostalgically of the golden days of Herod the Great and relishes the idea of a stable Judaea so her troops can be better utilized in the conquest of more abundant lands. She would be ready to view the ruler of such a nation more as an ally than a subject."

Joseph stood up and covered his face with the chin flap of his turban.

"So you see, my lord, just by being who you are, you will create the Jewish kingdom and save the world."

Jesus sat speechless. Joseph signaled the two soldiers to ready the horses.

"It is late. I see your uncle Clopas is ready for breakfast. I am sure you have a lot to think about. I will meet you again at your mother's home in Cana."

Jesus rose to accept the masked kisses of the nobleman and struggled to say something. Nothing came out. When they had gone, he returned to his bed and fell into a fitful sleep.

CHAPTER FIVE

The next day John saw Jesus coming to him, and he said, Behold the Lamb of God who takes away the sin of the world!

—John 1:29

Despite the complexities of the conspiracy, Jesus's role at first would be relatively simple. To take advantage of the momentum of expectation caused by his cousin John, Jesus would appear publicly before him for baptism. He would pose as a Nazarite. Then (barring complications which might arise owing to the unpredictability of the mad Baptizer), Jesus would take over John's disciples and gather as many new followers as he could as he walked back to Galilee and his mother's estate in Cana, near Nazareth.

More of a compound than a residence, the Cana property originally housed a Roman equestrian training facility. Wise Joseph had acquired it before Jesus was born and converted the stables to living quarters for his woodworkers and their families. It was estimated that the facility could comfortably house up to one hundred people. It would be the perfect venue for a monastic-styled "school" to house the host of new devotees and students who would inevitably form around Jesus the teacher.

The difficult task of transforming John's former followers and the multitude of new devotees into a religious-political presence would be the responsibility of twelve Carmelite monks handpicked by the Mount Carmel abbot. These twelve were designated "beloved disciples." They would serve at first as Jesus's bodyguards and also conduct baptisms and arrange the myriad details of a tightly choreographed mass movement.

The spectacle of a "prophetically correct" public entry of Jesus into Jerusalem had been carefully choreographed by Joseph of Ramtha and a committee of seven elders. They estimated it would take at least three years to "fatten the flock" (as Clopas put it), during which time Jesus would circulate throughout the area to cultivate his public persona and establish his spiritual credentials.

"The people. They are our army," Uncle Clopas never tired of saying. "They are so many—many more than even Pilate could easily crush if ever they dreamed one dream."

This phase of the Plan would require the utmost delicacy. Jesus would be exposed to intense scrutiny by the leaders of all the sects. He would inevitably be challenged by the Dead Sea Essenes who passively supported John but who considered their Mount Carmel counterparts fornicators and "seekers after smooth things." Jesus would have to fire their imaginations without tempting any of them to prematurely endorse or denounce his "ministry."

A week before departing Ramtha, Jesus was visited by his mother, Mary, who, since Joseph's death twelve years earlier, resided most of the time at the Cana estate. She appeared uneasy as she listened to the particulars of the Plan but was thrilled to learn that her son would soon be staying with her.

Word reached Clopas that John had publicly blasphemed before the Pharisees and was arrested and briefly imprisoned by Herod's men. He was released with the warning that next time arrest would mean his death. Nevertheless, he returned directly to Aenon and continued to baptize. It was time for Jesus to confront his deranged cousin, steal his disciples, and trigger the chain of events that would make him King of the Jews.

Reluctantly, Jesus took leave of his uncle and set out on foot. To ensure he had the appearance of a wandering holy man, he took only water and avoided the main roads, traveling instead by wilderness paths north into Samaria. Turning east, he skirted the foothills of Mount Gerizim and walked through rugged country to the flatlands of the Jordan Valley. It took four days to reach Aenon on the west side of the river a few miles east of Scythopolis.

As he neared the river, he came upon small groups of men and women who appeared to be lost in reverie. Some sat quietly upon the ground; others stood and rocked back and forth in a grotesque dance. Most of them hummed mindlessly or mumbled scraps of scripture. "Followers of John," he thought. "My future disciples."

He rounded a small stand of junipers and found himself confronted by a naked and emaciated figure standing directly in his path. He had never seen such a creature, not even among the dung-eating hermits of Arad. Its filth-caked hair and beard nearly reached its waist, and its skin was so layered with dirt that it was hard to determine its age or race. Only the eyes, which burned like twin coals, testified to a life within the wretched, stinking shell. It held what appeared to be the jawbone of an ass or horse and shook it threateningly at Jesus.

"Their slain also shall be cast out, and the stink of their corpses shall come up, and the mountains shall be drenched with their blood!"

The voice was painfully shrill, but the accent was that of a well-educated man, perhaps even an aristocrat. Jesus sidestepped the old man and continued on his way. Suddenly the back of his head exploded with pain, and he found himself blinded and face down on the sand fighting for consciousness. As he struggled to get up, he realized that the old man had jumped on him from behind and was beating him with the jawbone.

"The sword of the Lord is filled with blood, it is made fat with the blood, and with the fatness of lambs and goats, with the fat of the kidneys of rams!"

Weakened from four days of fasting, Jesus nonetheless managed to roll over and pin the old man to the ground. Appearing disgustingly delighted at this switch of positions, the mad hermit laughed hysterically and ground his filthy groin hard against Jesus.

"And unicorns shall fall with them, and bullocks with the bulls; and the land shall be soaked with their blood, and the soil enriched with their fatness!"

A crowd of pilgrims rushed to the scene and mumbled their disgust at what appeared at first glance to be Jesus's sexual assault of a skeletal hermit. His head throbbing with pain, Jesus managed to jump to his feet and stumble down the path. His babbling "victim" lay writhing on his back in the dust, thrashing his arms and legs like an overturned scarab.

"For it is the day of the Lord's vengeance and the year of recompense for the cause of Zion! All the fat is the Lord's! All the fat is the Lord's!"

"These are the disciples I must snatch from John?" he thought. "The scriptures should never have been placed in the hands of such as these. To exorcise a demon, they would evoke the devil." Jesus began to doubt the wisdom of "liberating" these fanatics.

The pounding in his head soon subsided, and a cool wisp of air told Jesus he was nearing the river. The path became crowded with devotees coming for baptism. He wondered if John would recognize him. He quickened his pace and passed a small group of pilgrims. Their hostile reaction made him realize that, even though the river was not yet in sight, he was already in the queue to be baptized.

Lustration was an ancient ritual that was not limited to Semites. Full-body immersion in water not only assured the bodily cleanliness of the worshipper but also served as a declaration of spiritual renewal—a rebirth. Converts to Judaism in foreign countries had been initiated into the faith by water baptism since the days of Hillel the Great. At home the Hebrews institutionalized this procedure to an elaborate degree. All who wished to enter the Temple had to first cleanse themselves in the waters of the mikvah, a ritual well dug next to the exterior wall of the Temple. Each worshipper was required to descend the steps of the mikvah and immerse completely. A priest was positioned to assure that even the tips of the worshipper's hair had been submerged. Satisfied that the devotee had been properly immersed, the priest shouted "Kosher!"[9] and awaited the next entrant.

The very act of John performing baptism rituals in the river Jordan could easily be interpreted as a heretical slap in the face to the Temple establishment. In John's scenario, Israel was the Temple, the holy river was its mikvah, and he was the only high priest spiritually qualified to declare its people "kosher." Jesus knew that once he assumed leadership of John's revolution there would be no turning back.

The line snaked its way gradually toward the river from midmorning to late afternoon before Jesus caught sight of the baptismal pool. Here the waters of the Jordan flowed almost black with silt and the filthy debris from every town and village along its winding path from the Sea of Galilee. Still, after standing hours in the sun, the water looked inviting.

At last, Jesus saw John standing torso-deep in the water. He appeared to be naked, but it was impossible to tell. Thick black hair

---

9. In Hebrew, the letters Kaf-Shin-Resh, meaning "pure or ritualistically fit."

covered nearly every inch of his body, even his shoulders and back. Devotees approached him in a single line. He mumbled briefly to each of them before bending them roughly backward beneath the surface of the muddy waters. Returning them erect, he presented them with a small white river rock, then mumbled something in their ears and sent them on their way.

At last, it was Jesus's turn. He unwrapped his dusty outer garment and waded directly toward John, whose eyes were closed in prayer. Jesus stood directly in front of John and waited for him to open his eyes. When he did, he immediately recognized his cousin. His tired face seemed to burst with madness and disbelief. He opened his mouth wide, displaying the most appallingly foul-smelling remains of blackened teeth.

"Welcome, cousin. Have you come to save me from myself—or just the world?"

Jesus spoke so that all standing on the riverbank could hear. "I have come to be baptized." He made every effort to maintain eye contact with John, but it was difficult because his feet were slowly sinking into the soft sand, and he was forced to continually shift his weight back and forth as he alternately pulled each foot free.

"Listen to you!" John sneered. "Straight from your school on the mountain and already you roar like the Lion of Judah. Perhaps you should baptize me!"

The last thing in the world Jesus wanted was to enter into a public debate with John.

"I have come to be baptized," Jesus said, this time loud enough for even more to hear. John waded close to Jesus and seized his cousin by the arms.

"You are *still* a little bastard," he hissed. Pulling Jesus close, he put his stinking mouth to his cousin's ear. "It is too late, my bastard Lord. The Plan is dead. I have birth-strangled it. I promise them more than an earthly king could ever deliver. The nation is beyond healing. The vitals rot, and the stink outrages the nostrils of God. The body is dead, cousin, and I only have a moment to save the soul."

While looking into John's mad eyes, Jesus, for a moment, believed John's words. Surely, the Plan *was* madness. It could never succeed. Then his thoughts went blank as if sucked from his brain by John's gaze. Jesus stood dumb and bewitched, tumbling into the dark pools of his cousin's eyes. Seeing this, the crowd on shore began to speculate excitedly among themselves. "What are they saying? Why is John taking so much time with this Nazarite? Could this be his master? Could this be the moment of our deliverance?"

John's face softened. He broke his gaze and kissed Jesus on the cheek. For the first time in his life, Jesus was not afraid of him.

"Go back to your school, cousin. Copy the scriptures and bury them safely. Or take your mother back to Egypt. Seek the 'smooth things' in the time that remains. The dream has passed. My time is short, and if you set your foot upon this path, they will lead you like a lamb to the altar."

"Perhaps," Jesus whispered. But as his wits returned, he knew there was no decision for him to make. The momentum of the Plan was too ponderous. He could not stop it now any more than he could reverse the flow of the river which now formed a waving vesica around the two kinsmen. Couldn't John see that? Why was he making it so hard?

"I am sorry, John. Please let us embrace our roles and get on with it."

John's eyes narrowed, and he began to pant violently. He tightened his grip on Jesus's arms and squeezed them painfully to his side. In one move, he kicked Jesus's feet out from under him and plunged him into the water. The crowd at the water's edge exploded into panic as they realized that John, too, had disappeared beneath the water's surface. Jesus struggled to free himself from John's grip, but it was no use. John sank his knee into his cousin's chest and attempted to knock the air out of his lungs, but Jesus twisted his body and managed a solid kick to John's groin. Free at last, Jesus tried to reach the surface for air but found himself forced under by John's firm grip on the back of his neck. Water was now in his lungs, and he was completely disoriented and hysterical. Suddenly he felt himself thrust up through the surface. John shook him like a wet rag. He tried to gasp for air, but for a moment could only manage to cough up great spurts of water. John held his helpless cousin up by his hair before the stunned crowd. Jesus's arms flailed wildly in the air.

"Behold!" John's voice thundered across the water. The sky became a riot of birds, frightened from their cool perches by the bellowing prophet. The crowd instantly fell silent; many dropped to their knees. "Behold! The Lamb of God, who takes away the sin of the world!"

CHAPTER SIX

For this same Herod had sent out and arrested John and cast him
into prison, because of Herodias, wife of his brother Philip, whom
he had married. For John had said to Herod, It is not lawful for you
to marry your brother's wife.

—Mark 6:17–18

Jesus coughed the last dregs of water from his lungs and became
painfully conscious that he was being held up by his own hair. The
multitude at the water's edge was silent and visibly confused.

"The Plan dies here," Jesus thought. "This mob will stone me to
death."

Then John released him. His feet touched the sandy river bottom,
and he struggled awkwardly toward the bank.

"Behold the Lamb of God!" John repeated, his voice ringing over
the surface of the water with such sarcastic clarity that those standing
in line far out of sight of the baptismal pool heard and wondered.

"Behold the Lamb of God!"

Jesus continued to wade out of the pool.

"Behold the Lamb of God!" With each mocking repetition, John's
voice became more subdued and mournful until it finally seemed to
transmit in its haunting timbre the sorrow of the whole world.

"Behold...the Lamb..." Then John turned his head to heaven and shouted, "Father! Heli! Joseph! Behold your beloved Son! I hope you are well pleased!"

Jesus pulled himself from the pool and gathered up his outer garment. He wanted to run but feared the crowd would follow and kill him. Staring for a moment into their faces, he wondered how his father would feel if he could see him like this. Perhaps he would want him to die like a king—like an ancient ritual king of Greece or Thrace—torn to pieces by his people, who then would eat his flesh and sprinkle his blood upon the fields to assure the land's fertility. The thought amused him. Why not? What did he have to lose? At this point, what else could he offer? *A Perfect Master does not dread life, for he knows there is no dread afterlife.*

"I will tell you a great truth." He pointed his finger at John, who was now weeping and wading upstream out of sight. "Among those born of women there has not risen anyone greater than John the Baptist. Yet he who is least in the coming kingdom will be greater than he. Here am I—if you would have a king."

What a stupid thing to say! He regretted it the moment he said it. But to his utter amazement, those immediately in front of him fell to their knees. Others followed, then others, until finally all but a few knelt before the King of the Jews.

Jesus would never see his cousin John again.

From that moment, the Plan proceeded precisely as the elders had envisioned. John, for the moment, had disappeared and no longer posed a threat to anyone but himself. In the blink of an eye, Jesus, the mystery Nazarite whom John had proclaimed the "Lamb of God," assumed the mastership of nearly all of his cousin's disciples. Scores more who heard the story of the baptism joined them and followed the king north to Galilee.

The retinue was intercepted on the road near Jericho by the twelve Carmelite beloved disciples, who quietly became part of the throng and surreptitiously took control. Jesus recognized them all, but he was most surprised and delighted to see among them Brother Apollonius, the master physician and his friend and mentor for eleven years. Young Lazar, the abbot's personal valet, was also among the Carmelite agents. The lad was only sixteen years old but had pleaded with the abbot to be made part of the great "Messiah adventure." The old man agreed on the condition that Lazar would be his eyes and ears on all matters that might affect Carmelite interests.

As the troop snaked its way north, Jesus tried his hand at public speaking. He taught simple clichés of Essene wisdom, which were seized upon and devoured by the people as doctrines of the new kingdom. Not wishing to prematurely antagonize either Roman or Jewish authorities, he limited his public acts to simple healing and philanthropic gestures rather than political statements or miracles. Everything he said and did was amplified and interpreted for the people by the beloved disciples. Jesus soon learned exactly what Uncle Clopas meant by "fattening the flock."

By the time they arrived in Cana, the entourage had swollen to nearly fifty men and women who had renounced the world and pledged absolute fealty to their new spiritual master. Fortunately, Mary's estate was large enough to accommodate this many and more. With the help of the beloved disciples, they were baptized and gently introduced to the order and light disciplines of a layperson's monastic routine. Everything, it seemed, was proceeding on schedule.

Shortly after Jesus's return to Cana, he received a visit from Joseph of Ramtha, Uncle Clopas, and five key conspirators. After the coup, this Council of Seven would act as the king's ministers and executors of political, military, and economic policy. Jesus was overwhelmed by the details of the plot. It appeared nothing was left to chance. It was at this meeting that he learned how much of the Plan revolved around the violent activities of the Zealators. Assassinations had already been carried out upon low-level members of Herod's government and the Temple bureaucracy. People were already dying so that his bloodline could once again reign.

Late in the afternoon, Mary interrupted the meeting, saying that an angel[10] had arrived with news from Sepphoris, the capital city of King Herod Antipas. The young man's name was Perez, the youngest son of Elam of Japhia, one of the council members. He was ushered immediately into the study chamber.

"My lords, two days ago I was hard by when John the son of Zechariah was arrested by Herod's soldiers and placed in the grotto cells across from the temple of Augustus. I secreted myself in the stable adjoining the cells and could see and hear much that transpired. Furthermore, as astonishing as this may sound to my lords, last night he was secretly visited by Herod's own wife, Herodias, who, possessed by a demon of lust unimaginably foul, unveiled herself before the Baptizer's prison gate and promised him his freedom if he would lie with her that night. John teased her with soft words of Solomon's Song, and when she swooned, he spat upon her nakedness and cursed her most vehemently. The wrathful harlot then gathered her garments and vowed that she would have the Nazarite's head. I spoke with him only briefly, then I hastened here."

After a few questions from his father, Perez was dismissed with the council's gratitude and given food and a room for the night.

Joseph of Ramtha was the first to respond. "Brethren, this is indeed sad news, but it has little to do with our work here. We all know that Zechariah's dear boy was destined by temperament for

---

10. The word *angel* in Hebrew means "messenger, courier, or the bearer of news" and is applied to both mortal and celestial beings.

martyrdom. He has done his work and made straight the road for our savior. His spark flashed brightly but has now spent its fuel. Let us seek not to entangle ourselves in the dangerous details of his inevitable conclusion."

Everyone eventually agreed that John's troubles were self-inflicted and that the Plan would only be jeopardized by any attempts to intervene on his behalf. Jesus remained silent. The council broke up after deciding that it was time for Jesus to enhance his public persona by initiating a campaign of beneficent acts, miracles, and healing. The details were to be left to Jesus and the Carmelite disciples.

That night, Jesus could not sleep. He wanted to know more about John. Carrying a tiny oil lamp, he made his way to the servants' quarters and awakened the exhausted angel. He questioned the young man until dawn about every detail of the arrest. He especially wanted to know the exact words John spoke to the boy after Herod's wife withdrew.

"He spoke of you, my lord." Perez hesitated as if he feared an angel's life depended upon delivering only good news. "He said he would precede you in death as he did in life. Then he laughed most pathetically. He bade me draw near the grated door and whispered, 'Ask my cousin—are you truly he that should come?' Then, with the words of the prophet Isaiah, he lamented, 'I have trodden the winepress alone, and of the people there was none with me.'"

Jesus sat silently for a few moments. Then he startled the boy with his words. "Return to Sepphoris and carry this message to John: 'Peace be with you, cousin. Make straight our way to paradise.'"

"Yes, my lord. 'Peace be with you, cousin. Make straight our way to paradise.'"

Jesus thanked him and quietly returned to his room.

BOOK TWO

MARRIAGE AT CANA

CHAPTER ONE

The bandits who were crucified with him were also reproaching him.
—Matthew 27:44

Jesus shook the cross with a powerful body spasm and pulled at the ropes until the flesh of his wrists tore. He was breathing again, but now in loud tortured gasps that made his torso a billow of skin and ribs. He rolled his head violently right and left. Suddenly his abdomen contracted so deeply into the cavity of his frail body that Lazar thought for a moment he could see his spine. Then, while his head was turned, an amber vomit of vinegar and gall shot from his mouth with such force that it splattered the nail-pierced feet of the man crucified to his right.

"Messiah! Why don't you jump down and get me a napkin?" he croaked at Jesus.

"Shut your mouth! This is the man who would deliver us all!" shouted the other. He twisted his head to look upon Jesus. He could not. Neither of the condemned could see the center cross. "Master, remember me when you come into your kingdom."

Through thick clouds of pain that shrouded his every thought, Jesus heard a weakened echo of his own voice, once

again mustering his old Essene bedside manner to comfort the
poor fellow. "Today you will be with me in paradise."

In the days that followed the meeting with the angel from Sepphoris, Jesus fell into a dark mood. He stopped taking his meals and
barred his chamber door against visitors. His quarters on the second
floor of the villa overlooked the courtyard and well. Steps led from
his bedchamber to the roof where he brooded in the cool of the evening. It was here that he chose to spend the nights of late spring in
solitude.

During his absence, the beloved disciples continued to baptize
and teach, all the while assuring the growing body of pupils that their
Lord was deep in prayer. Besides the twelve Carmelites, there were
now seventy-two full-time resident pupils. Mary was deeply concerned that without the presence of the master the neophytes would
soon become discouraged, or worse. The Council of Seven also grew
impatient for Jesus to begin the next phase of the Plan. Ephron of
Arbela grumbled that Jesus's first miracle would need to be his own
exorcism.

On the twelfth day of his fast, Jesus, bored with his own melancholy, roused himself before dawn. He washed his face and hands,
then knelt near the eastern wall of his rooftop hermitage. Vowing
silently not to rise until the spirit of his inmost will revealed a plan of
action, Jesus closed his eyes and prepared to battle the demons that
torment all who would attain perfect stillness: external sounds, body
aches, and the most formidable devil of all, the wandering mind.

At the monastery, Jesus had delighted in meditation. "How can
you hope to touch the heart of God if your own heart remains undis-
covered?" was the favorite adage of his meditation master. As the
sun rose, Jesus was assailed with the chaotic noises of awakening vil-

lage life—first from his own home, then from throughout the compound. Finally, it seemed there was no sound in all of Cana that did not intrude upon his stillness. He could not ignore the drama being played out at the door of his mother's kitchen.

"Good day m-m-my lady."

"Good day, Nathaniel. Won't you come in and breakfast with us?"

"Thank you, m-m-m-my lady, bu-bu-but I cannot. I come as the angel of my m-m-m-master, Aaron Ben Yehuda, who has sent me to deliver g-g-good tidings of great joy, and to ext-t-tend to you, your f-f-family, and all of your household a joy-joy-joy-joyous invitation."

"Indeed?" Mary pretended not to notice the poor boy's stutter.

"His m-m-m-message is thus: 'To m-m-Mary, the esteemed wi-wi-widow of Joseph the ga-ga-ga-Great Carpenter, b-b-blessings and p-p-peace. I, Aaron b-b-Ben Yehuda, give thanks to gaw-gaw-gaw-God that he has allowed me to l-l-l-live long and has blessed my eye-eye-eyes so they m-m-might see the day of the marriage of my youngest da-da-daughter d-d-Dinah to the noble wo-wo-widower Isaac Ben Samuel. I humbly be-be-seech you, your children, and gr-gr-grandchildren, and all who dwa-dwell within your g-g-gates to honor my house with your pa-pa-presence at the feast that will fa-fa-follow the nu-nuu-nuuu-n-nuptial solem-em-em-nities in the cooling shade of my fru-fruit orchard hard by my home n-n-nine days hence on the twenty-s-s-seventh day of sssssssss-Sivan at the sixth hour.'"

"Slow down, dear boy. Does your master know that my son Jesus, the teacher, and *four score* of his disciples currently reside here in our home?"

"Ahhh...ahhhhh...I am sure he d-d-does, my-my lady."

"And are you quite sure your master's invitation extends to so great a number?"

"His me-me-message says, 'all who dwa-dwa-dwell within your gates,' my la-la-lady. Pa-pa-please, my lady—my master is a p-p-proud man and will pa-pa-punish me if he believes my awk-awk-awkward delivery of this ma-ma-message o-o-off-offends you and gives you ca-ca-cause to refuse his invitation. If I may be fa-fa-frank, my lady, you are the na-na-noblest of the aristo-cra-crats of our province. Your pres-presence will bring g-g-g-great honor to his house."

"Go back to your master and tell him that 'Mary, the widow of Joseph Ben Heli, rejoices in his happiness and will be honored to attend the wedding feast of his daughter Dinah and Isaac Ben Samuel.' Also tell your master, 'She will relay this glad word to her sons Simon, Joses, Judas, and James and their families who reside in Sidon and Bethlehem, and to her daughter, Leah, and her husband in Nazareth. But before she further extends the invitation to her son Jesus, the teacher, and the *four score* disciples under his spiritual tutelage, she asks for confirmation that his goodwill shall not be strained by the addition of so great a multitude.'"

"Thank you, my la-la-lady. I will re-retur-return with my m-m-master's reply."

Jesus abandoned all pretense of meditation and drifted into the musings of a common eavesdropper.

"Aaron Ben Yehuda," he thought, "the biggest hypocrite in Galilee."

After the death of Joseph, it was Aaron Ben Yehuda who produced fraudulent documents that allegedly proved that Joseph had deeded over certain land holdings, including the Cana estate. The old fool grossly underestimated the family's influence and Mary's business acumen. Eventually he was nearly prosecuted himself for forgery over the incident. Jesus knew the old miser would renege on the wedding invitation after he discovered how many more mouths he would have to feed. Eighty more would more than double the guest list. The extra wine alone would cost him a fortune—not that the old thief couldn't afford it. Jesus loitered in his own ill temper. "Oh, to see his face when eighty more dinner guests arrive. That would delight all of Cana!" Jesus laughed out loud.

Suddenly the thought of food and wine pierced his bowels. They growled like fighting dogs. He had not eaten in twelve days. The hunger made him feel human again. Forget the meditation. He must eat. He slowly got up and carefully descended the steps to his room and dressed for breakfast. The dark night of the soul had passed.

He broke his fast with grapes, figs, and water, but was full after only a few bites. Mary was overjoyed at her son's resurrection and strangled him with hugs as she chattered of her twelve days of worry. Weak as he was, he instructed that word be passed to the disciples that the master would teach this afternoon and asked that appointments with council members be prioritized and scheduled.

After his breakfast, he retired to the baths to steam away the poisons that twelve days of fasting had leached to the surface of his skin. As a special treat, his mother sent two of her own servants to oil his body and scrape his skin. He hadn't been oiled and scraped in years. For a moment, Jesus really did feel like a king.

———

"Nathaniel! Dear child, what happened to your face?"

"I fa-fa-fa-fell upon the steps of my ma-ma-master's porch, my-my-lady. It is nothing. I bring a wri-wri-written message of reply from my ma-master."

Mary did not believe the poor lad. He had been beaten. She took the delicately written scroll from Nathaniel's quivering hand and unrolled it.

"To Mary, the esteemed widow of Joseph Ben Heli, blessings and peace. I rejoice that you and members of your noble family will celebrate with me my daughter's wedding. Please know also that I would grieve deeply if your son Jesus and the entire community of his students did not also attend. It was always my intention that it be so, and I apologize that my servant's ineptitude has caused you confusion."

Mary gently touched the boy's battered face. "Thank your master and tell him I will extend the invitation to all within our gates."

"Thank you, my lady."

————

For a few days, Jesus was happy to put aside the anxiety of the plot and simply play the part of a teacher. It was a role he often fantasized playing at the monastery. He was good at it. He gave silent thanks to his Carmelite masters, who for eighteen years were so insistent that he memorize the Torah and the works of the prophets. Every word from his mouth was weighed against scripture even by the humblest seeker. He knew the Sadducees and Pharisees would present a much more difficult challenge.

In the evenings, he chatted on the roof with Brother Apollonius or joined in with the members of his family who had begun arriving from afar to attend the wedding feast. Everyone thought it was uproariously funny that Aaron Ben Yehuda would be forced to pay for the food and drink of over eighty extra guests.

Jesus's half-brother Simon, who was now a successful wine broker in Sidon, had a particularly delicious piece of gossip. "My associate in Tyre tells me that Aaron Ben Yehuda sent word that he desperately needed *eighteen* firkins of the finest Chalybon and would pay whatever premium necessary to have them delivered in time for the wedding feast."

Simon was almost in tears from laughter. "The request was on such short notice that my friend did not have sufficient amphorae to transport such a quantity and was forced to ship the nectar in bulk in six huge stone pots. It is costing him a fortune. The deposit on the pots cost nearly as much as the wine!"

"At least at the feast we will get the Chalybon," James interjected. "I know for a fact he plans to serve the other guests that Sorrentine swill that was rejected last winter by Herod's wine master."

"Before he sent it back, I heard he had the father of Herodias pickled alive in it." Judas always had a mind for the macabre.

Joses added with an air of mock erudition, "At least the old forger will probably add so much water that it will not poison anyone."

"You can be sure that Isaac Ben Samuel will be served the good stuff," Mary contributed with uncharacteristic mirth. "Even though old Ben Yehuda pays the bill, it is still the bridegroom's party."

Jesus had never seen his family in such a lighthearted mood. During his eighteen years at the monastery, he had visited their various homes only a handful of times, and not since he was eleven had he seen them all together.

On the eve of the great wedding feast, he managed to break away and take a peaceful stroll with his sister, Leah, now twenty-six, and her eight-year-old daughter, Sarah. When the child was out of earshot, Leah seized Jesus's hand and stopped him.

"You lied to me when we were children," she chided. "You told me you were not a king."

"But Simon told you the truth," Jesus said seriously. "Soldiers can still kill us."

"It's not too late. I believe you don't want this. You are a healer, not a king. James is stronger. None of the sects call him 'bastard.' He told me he feels called—"

Their conversation was interrupted by the unexpected appearance of Uncle Clopas, who, after nearly smothering Leah with kisses and hugs, rambled on embarrassingly about what a beautiful young woman she had become. Reluctantly releasing his niece, he apologized for interrupting and begged her for a few minutes of her brother's time. She gently touched Clopas upon the cheek. "Of course, Uncle." She called little Sarah, who tugged her hand and pulled her down the path toward the main house. "Think about what I said, brother. It's not too late."

"Not too late for what?" Clopas asked.

"Family intrigue. Nothing important. So, you've come for the wedding?"

Clopas rubbed his hands in anticipation. "Would not miss it for the world. So, Aaron the forger will at last be rid of his youngest daughter?"

"Yes, and our miniature monastery will swell the guest list of the wedding feast by over four score!"

They both shared a moment of shameless laughter.

"My half-brother Simon tells us the old goat was forced to purchase an additional eighteen firkins of fine Chalybon wine just for the extra guests!"

Clopas stopped smiling for a moment and then broke into such a fit of laughter that he began coughing uncontrollably and had to be helped to a nearby bench.

Catching his breath, he managed to spit out a few words before the laughing-coughing cycle resumed. "All that wine—and you and your eighty Nazarites won't touch a drop!"

Jesus had completely forgotten himself. Since his appearance before John for baptism, he presented himself to the world as a Nazarite holy man. He could no more drink wine in public than touch a menstruating woman or eat the flesh of swine. Jesus now joined his uncle in a crippling laugh as he speculated about how best to spring the expensive news on Aaron Ben Yehuda.

"Come, Uncle, if I cannot drink to the bride tomorrow, we must toast to her happiness tonight!"

"Verily, my lord, not since Solomon has such wisdom prevailed."

As the two kinsmen walked back toward the house, they paused for a moment on high ground to enjoy the cool air. From the west, the direction of Aaron Ben Yehuda's land, the breeze carried the frightened last cry of a lamb as its throat was cut.

"Sounds like the guests will have plenty to eat as well," giggled Clopas. "Yes, my royal nephew, tomorrow will be a memorable day."

CHAPTER TWO

On the third day there was a marriage feast in Cana, a city of Galilee;
and the mother of Jesus was there. And Jesus and his disciples were
also invited to the marriage feast. And when the wine ran low, his
mother said to Jesus, They have no wine.

—John 2:1–3

Jesus rose at midnight. He bathed and dressed, then meditated for
nearly an hour on the roof. On this morning, he called the beloved
disciples together long before the pupils awoke for dawn devotionals. There was an air of great excitement because the wedding would
provide an excellent opportunity to enhance his public image.

To add an atmosphere of mystery, it was decided that Jesus and
his entourage would not attend the wedding ceremony itself but
appear *en masse* at the feast after the other guests had arrived. Brother
Apollonius suggested that Jesus conspicuously offer a benediction or
otherwise bless the bride and groom. Everyone would be instructed
before they left the compound that they were to watch the master
very closely and follow his example as to where to sit, what to eat and
drink, and other matters of social decorum.

As was customary, a master of ceremonies, or chief guest, hired
by the father of the bride (but officially in service to the bridegroom)
would preside over the wedding feast. Lazar had discovered that

on this day the role would be filled by Mordecai Ben Nahor, one of Aaron Ben Yehuda's brothers-in-law and for many years his solicitor and crony in business.

"How two old scorpions have avoided stinging each other to death for so long is verily a miracle," Jesus joked. "Instruct the pupils to respectfully pay heed to the master of ceremonies but ultimately to look to me for guidance."

Jesus joined the general assembly for the dawn devotionals and afterward preached on the subject of marriage—its place in society and the parallels to God and his people and a king and his country. There was genuine affection forming among the pupils. Jesus marveled at the sublime efficiency of the Carmelite disciplinary system and thought to himself that it would not be long before he would look upon many of them as beloved disciples.

Mary also was up early, preparing bridal gifts and treating herself to the sweet company of Leah, her daughters-in-law, and grandchildren. They and Jesus's brothers would attend the wedding ceremony itself. All the excitement was a welcome distraction from the tensions of the great Plan.

Midmorning, Jesus withdrew from the company of disciples and family and retired to his room for a calming hour of meditation and breathing exercises. After what seemed like only a few minutes, he was jolted from his trance by a knock at his door and the voice of Lazar calling him to the marriage feast.

———

"Jesus! Jesus Ben Heli! Look at you! A man...a holy man. Mordecai! Come, greet the son of Joseph the Great Carpenter. Rabbi, forgive me, I have always thought of you as my own son! It has been so long, forgive me. Mordecai! Mordecai! Where is our master of ceremonies?"

This was the moment Jesus was dreading the most. Aaron Ben Yehuda couldn't have been more offensively patronizing. As if on cue, Mordecai Ben Nahor appeared behind the father of the bride looking absolutely oily.

"Come. Come! You honor my house. Mordecai will show you and all your lovely students to your seats in the orchard. Lovely day, yes? You honor my house on this glad day...glad day. Ah, but first...if it be God's will...be pleased to meet my new son-in-law, the noble and *prosperous* Isaac Ben Samuel, who has this day wed my dear, dear Dinah. You remember Dinah...the last of my doves."

Jesus turned to bless the couple but was visibly startled when he observed the obscene disparity between their ages. The bride could not have seen more than fourteen summers, while Isaac Ben Samuel was an enfeebled septuagenarian. Ignoring decorum, Jesus took the hand of the bride and squeezed it in sympathy. He then held his hands in blessing over the couple.

"They who have united this day as man and woman, let fall success! May hearts and flesh unite to bring forth bliss, prosperity, and progeny." Jesus thought he would choke on the words.

Polite applause followed the blessing, then Mordecai Ben Nahor quickly ushered Jesus to his family's table and seated him next to Mary. Rows of tables had been positioned under the impressive stand of date palms for the crowd of pupils, who seemed anxious to begin enjoying themselves.

Jesus was now relaxed. The entrance went well. The disciples and pupils were nearby, and, with the exception of the sad fate of the bride, it looked like it was going to be a pleasant afternoon.

Jesus looked around at all the activity. In spite of his miserly reputation, Aaron Ben Yehuda certainly had not spared any expense for this occasion. A dozen maids scurried from table to table with cool water and trays of delicacies, and the air was filled with music. Not far from the table, against the shaded side of the well that served to irrigate the orchard, Jesus spied six enormous stone pots with heavy wooden lids.

"The Chalybon from Damascus," he whispered in Mary's ear.

The thought made him smile but reminded him of his next duty. He had better break the news to the master of ceremonies before his followers got ideas about what to drink. Just then a young woman appeared at the table carrying a large pitcher of wine. Mary and the other members of his family gladly held out their cups, but when she neared Jesus, he held up his hand in refusal. Seeing this gesture, the din of the celebration became muffled, then stilled completely. It was so quiet that Jesus did not need to raise his voice to be heard.

"Be careful of kings who drink wine; and of princes who drink strong drink."

Perfect! When in doubt, quote Proverbs. He was proud of himself. He looked over to see broad smiles on the faces of Lazar and Brother Apollonius. The rest of the beloved disciples moved quickly to assure the servants that the followers of Jesus would be drinking water this day. The music resumed and the other guests continued their revelry.

Word of this change in menu immediately reached the master of ceremonies, who rushed to Aaron Ben Yehuda's table and whispered excitedly in his ear. Jesus was delighted to see his host's look of dismay and animated response to the news. All that expensive wine—at least the rest of the guests would now taste the finest wine in the world. A furious exchange of whispers then ensued, after which Aaron Ben Yehuda frantically summoned Ephraim, the overseer of servants. Some act of larceny was hatching in the greedy viper's imagination, Jesus thought. Turning his back to the guests, Aaron Ben Yehuda drew the man near and whispered new orders. Ephraim pulled away in astonishment, and Jesus saw him point questioningly toward the six stone pots near the well. His master quickly pulled Ephraim's hand down lest anyone notice and curtly dismissed him with a sweep of his own hand.

Delicious as the private joke was, Jesus got on with the business of "fattening the flock." He got up and walked among his disciples and the other guests, stopping and chatting at every table. Because of his reputation as a healer, conversations frequently turned to matters of health. Keeping Brother Apollonius inconspicuously near, Jesus ventured to diagnose the maladies of several of the wedding guests and extended to them invitations to visit the compound the following day for treatment.

The afternoon wore lazily on. The food continued to be delivered in waves, and more than a few guests were becoming delightfully drunk. Still, the six pots of fine wine rested unmolested near the well.

Suddenly the entire congregation turned to the east end of the orchard where a horseman had galloped to a stop, raising so much dust that he was greeted with groans and insults. It was Perez, the young angel from Sepphoris. Two beloved disciples immediately intercepted the lad and escorted him away from curious ears. Jesus knew something was terribly wrong. A few moments later, the boy led his horse toward the compound and the two disciples quietly returned to the feast and straight to Jesus's table. One put his mouth to the master's ear; the other shielded the scene from prying eyes.

"Lord, it grieves me to inform you that your cousin John is dead, beheaded last night upon Herod's order as a reward to his wife, Herodias, who compelled her daughter to seduce the drunken king. The head of the Baptizer was presented at Herod's birthday celebration, served to Herodias in a silver charger. The Council of Seven has called an emergency meeting this night at the Cana estate. We have been ordered not to leave your side."

Jesus did not acknowledge the message in any way but stared straight forward, to outward appearances as calm and motionless as a stone. Inwardly he reeled as if he had been struck in the chest. His mind, a swirling cauldron of disastrous scenarios, could not focus on a single thought long enough to react in any way.

"Lord? Lord? Did you not hear me? Perhaps we should leave the feast now. Plans must be made. My lord, are you ill?"

Jesus had to consciously force himself to take a breath. As he did, the happy din of the increasingly boisterous wedding guests became a nightmarish intrusion upon his private agony. It was the eighth hour, and a few of the more sober guests were already leaving the festivities. Aaron Ben Yehuda seemed anxious to encourage everyone to follow their example.

"Yes, goodnight, God bless you. Yes. It *is* getting late. Thank you. Yes, you honor my house—getting late—I know—I know—last of my doves."

The more intemperate guests, however, were showing no signs of leaving the festivities.

"I thirst! Wine! Aaron, tell your servants that our table needs more wine!"

"And our table too!"

"Another toast to the last of Aaron Ben Yehuda's doves!"

"The day is young. More wine! More wine!"

Suddenly Jesus became intensely conscious of his surroundings. He felt violated by every laugh, every shout. The feast was becoming as wild and chaotic as the turmoil in his own heart. Aaron Ben Yehuda and Mordecai huddled together and whispered. Several of the drunken guests grabbed serving girls and wrested the pitchers from their hands, smashing them to the ground when it was discovered they were empty.

"More wine! More wine! More wine!" The chant, begun at first by a handful of beardless bachelors, was picked up with a fury by the most intoxicated troublemakers, who accentuated the chorus by pounding their fists upon the tables. "More wine! More wine! More wine!"

"Dear friends! Dear friends!" The voice was that of Mordecai Ben Nahor. "Please listen."

The master of ceremonies was helped atop a table at the very front of the assembly.

"Dear friends and neighbors. I know we all wish to thank our host, the noble groom Isaac Ben Samuel, and his most generous father-in-law, Aaron Ben Yehuda, for today's festivities."

"A toast to Isaac Ben Samuel and Aaron Ben Yehuda! More wine! More wine!" The chant threatened to resume in full force.

"Friends! We have feasted and rejoiced all afternoon, and our hosts pray that you will take this great bliss with you as you now joyously return to your homes!"

The mob would have none of it. The chanting resumed with a vengeance.

"Friends! Friends! Aaron Ben Yehuda shares your great joy, but Ephraim has just informed him that we have at last exhausted our bountiful supply of wine."

"But we have not touched the six vessels that rest near the well," shouted an observant old man. "Tap those and we shall all swim home!"

The assembly roared with laughter and chanting. Aaron Ben Yehuda quickly summoned three servants who, with considerable effort, helped him up onto the table to join Mordecai.

"Alas, my friends, those great jars are filled only with pure well water, which our family has pledged for the synagogue mikvah. Sweet friends, we have all had our fill of wine this day. Go home now with the gratitude and blessings of our family."

"That old serpent!" Mary fumed under her breath. "He plans to return the expensive wine and demand a refund of his money."

Aaron Ben Yehuda's appeal was successful. The chanting tapered to a drunken mumble, and the multitude reluctantly started to gather their things to depart. Jesus, too, had regained his composure and looked to his family and disciples for an expeditious exit. He stood up, flanked by two beloved disciples. He turned to Brother Apollonius, then to Mary. His face was so pale, they feared he would become ill. Then, to everyone's surprise, Jesus mounted the nearest table. The entire assembly turned in stunned amazement. "Brethren! Oracles are on the lips of the king."

It suddenly became so quiet Jesus could hear his heartbeat in his throat. Aiming his shaking finger at the six stone pots resting near the well, he erupted with a bellowing thunder that matched the mad roar of John the Baptist, "I can turn that water into wine!"

CHAPTER THREE

The chief guest tasted the water that had become wine.

—John 2:9

The disciples were visibly shaken. They had never seen the master in such a state. The bodyguards lunged toward the table to pull him down, but Mary ordered them to stand back.

Aaron Ben Yehuda cleared his throat and let out a nervous giggle. "Rabbi, you must be tired from the festivities. Surely—"

"Those great jars are filled with water?" Jesus's voice cracked with intensity.

"To the brim, rabbi."

"Then I shall turn it into wine!"

The father of the bride turned helplessly to his master of ceremonies. Fortunately, the blade of Mordecai Ben Nahor's guile sliced clean to the bone of the predicament. He knew it was no longer possible to keep the wine from the drunken revelers, and if he didn't play along with Jesus, he and Aaron Ben Yehuda would be exposed as miserly scoundrels, and the bridegroom would be dishonored.

"Rabbi, such a marvel has not been seen since the days of the prophets. Already the cup of our celebration overflows with the blessings your presence has brought to the house of Aaron Ben Yehuda!

How much greater the glory if it should now witness the touch of God's finger."

Mary stamped her foot and groaned in disgust.

Jesus did not reply but proceeded to leap from tabletop to tabletop until he reached the table of the father of the bride. Mordecai Ben Nahor hastened to help him down. Once on the ground, Jesus broke his grasp and walked straight to the well and the six great jars. The orchard exploded with the clamor of overturned tables and benches as the crowd climbed over one another to get a good view of what was about to take place. Even the disciples and pupils forgot their decorum and elbowed each other to see what the master would do. Mary was rescued from the chaos by Lazar and Brother Apollonius, who led her to the shelter of the servants' awning. The bodyguards pushed a path through the mob but could not get within arm's reach of their ward.

Jesus turned to Mordecai Ben Nahor and ordered him to loosen the leather straps that sealed the hardwood lid to one of the great vessels.

"Master of ceremonies! What do you see within the jar?"

At this point, Jesus had no doubt the old fraud would play his part.

Positioning his body so that no one but himself could see directly into the jar, Mordecai lifted the lid and gazed within.

"Water, Rabbi! Clear and sweet. I can see the bottom of the vessel." He quickly replaced the lid.

Picking up a carving knife from a serving tray, Jesus thrust it over his head as if to signal the start of a battle. "They who have ears to hear, let them hear! They who have eyes to see, let them see!"

Sweeping the knife down, he madly slashed at the six great pots, one by one, severing the leather sealing straps. No one moved. Jesus placed his foot upon the first vessel. "And all who thirst…let them drink!"

With that, he overturned the great jar with a violent kick, spilling its fragrant contents upon the ground and over the feet and ankles of those nearest the scene. Aaron Ben Yehuda's knees buckled, and he fell to the wine-soaked ground in a dead faint.

Mordecai Ben Nahor rushed to the other jars and threw off the lids. Dipping his hands inside one of them, he raised to his lips a pool of the blood-red ambrosia. "Wine! Wine! It's wine, my brethren! Heavenly wine, the best I have ever tasted! A miracle! Indeed, he has turned our water into wine!"

CHAPTER FOUR

This is the first miracle which Jesus performed in Cana of Galilee,
and thus he showed his glory; and his disciples believed in him.

—*John 2:11*

The wedding feast turned into an absolute riot. Drunken guests
trampled each other for the opportunity to plunge their heads
into the massive pots of wine. Jesus was seized by his guards and
swept from the orchard and back to the compound. Many of the
pupils joined wholeheartedly in the melee; others fled the scene or
fell to their knees in the wine-soaked mud, overcome with wonder.
Within minutes the uproar drew to Aaron Ben Yehuda's well every
uninvited resident of Cana.

It was midnight before a quorum of the Council of Seven reached
the Cana compound to discuss the death of John the Baptist. Joseph
of Ramtha was not among them. Hoping to reach the secret conclave
under the cover of darkness, they were assailed on the roads by stag-
gering revelers, who babbled of the miracle in Cana and the holy man
who turned water into wine from heaven.

The subcommittee assembled in Mary's kitchen. Ephron of
Arbela refused to sit.

"My boy, have you gone mad? We asked for miracles, not a riot!
With the Baptist dead, the eyes of the Pharisees will now seek out

the heir to his seditious mantle. We need a prince of peace, not street fakir."

Jesus said nothing.

"No, Ephron! It is you who are mad." Clopas was livid. "Can't you see? The timing could not have been better. An act of divine kindness at a humble wedding feast. This unassuming act *makes* him a prince of peace. You watch! You will see. It will endear him to the hearts of the common folk. Imagine! Heavenly wine to bless a simple wedding feast. It's perfect. Perfect! Why, it's almost *Dionysian*."

"Clopas is right," Elam of Japhia agreed. "News of both these events will be heard in tandem and interpreted as a single revelation. 'The offering is accepted,' the people will say. 'God has received the Baptist's blood and in return delivered unto us a wonder-working king!'"

"All of you, please. Be still!" Jesus stood up and looked down for a moment at his wine-stained hands and feet. "Is it not written that the Jews shall offer upon the altar *two* lambs—one in the morning and the other in the evening?"

No one knew what to say. Jesus remained standing, silently looking at his hands.

"My boy—"

Jesus stopped Clopas in mid-sentence. "My lords, the hour is late. Nothing will be decided until Joseph of Ramtha and the others can join our deliberations. That will take time. Please accept the hospitality of my mother's house this night. We will talk again in full assembly. Good night, my friends."

Only Clopas accepted the invitation. The others, too fearful of being seen in the daylight with the magician of Cana, departed almost immediately.

Elam was right. Within a week, the twin accounts of John's execution and the miracle at Cana raced from Caesarea to Gaza, conveyed by a thousand wags of the gossip's tongue.

"This is John the Baptist; he has risen from the dead! That is why miraculous powers are at work in him."

"It has begun. It is as Isaiah prophesied. John was the voice in the wilderness who heralded our savior, Jesus son of Joseph, of the royal house of David."

"The moment the Baptizer's head was severed, all the water turned to wine."

"John was Elijah reborn, and Jesus is his Elisha."

"John lives! His soul now dwells in the body of Jesus, the Davidian prince."

"I was at Aenon. I saw John baptize him. He called him the Lamb of God."

"He healed me of boils in Jericho. His voice is like honey and his hands soothe like balm."

"He could raise the dead with those hands."

BOOK THREE

KINGDOM COME

CHAPTER ONE

It came to pass when the people gathered around him to hear the word of God, he stood on the shore of the lake of Gennesaret.

—*Luke 5:1*

The morning after the wedding, Jesus arose before dawn and walked to the quarters of the beloved disciples. He awakened Brother Apollonius and Lazar, who quickly dressed and joined him in Mary's kitchen. They warmed themselves near the great clay oven and pondered their next move.

Brother Apollonius placed his hands on Jesus's shoulders. "My friend, I join you in mourning the death of your cousin. It is an ominous reminder of the gravity of our great endeavor. After yesterday's events, I think you will agree it would be unwise for you to remain much longer here at Cana. In fact, for the foreseeable future, I counsel that you do not sleep under the same roof two nights in succession."

"Are you suggesting I become a vagabond king?" Jesus chuckled.

"Who will be a vagabond king?" Uncle Clopas appeared in the doorway wrapped in a blanket.

"What better way to spread his fame, sir?" Lazar jumped up and offered his stool to Clopas.

"Brother Apollonius is right." Jesus slapped the tabletop. "By tomorrow night, the story of John's death and the wedding miracle

83

will find the ear of every Galilean. But the word must become flesh. Before the echo dies, I must reveal myself to the entire region. I cannot do it from behind the walls of a monastic community."

"Perhaps so, but we must wait until Joseph of Ramtha and the Council of Seven can be consulted." Clopas squirmed awkwardly on the tiny stool. "Besides, I know these people. They will be filled with the madness of expectation. You will be mobbed to death. You need first to speak to them in small groups—perhaps in the synagogues. Fatten the flock, yes! But first wait until they have become sheep. Is there something here we can eat?"

Jesus got up and poured a cup of goat's milk for his uncle. "I will speak in the synagogues. But I shall also address them by the thousands."

"Impossible!" snapped Clopas.

"Not impossible at all, Uncle. When I was a boy in Egypt, I was treated to a discourse on mathematics by Zosimus of Gade, the Neo-Pythagorean. The great man was over eighty and approaching death, but he acquiesced to the appeals of the academic community and agreed to deliver one last lecture in Alexandria.

"In addition to the nearly two thousand local students for whom the event was scheduled, nearly twice that number of foreign scholars poured into Alexandria to hear him speak. Unfortunately, no building in the city could be found to accommodate such a multitude—not even the magnificent Serapeum. The organizers suggested that the great man deliver his dissertation at the hippodrome, but Zosimus was too weak and his voice too soft to make such a venue suitable. Instead, he suggested a most unusual remedy.

"He gave instructions to gather the audience on the westernmost end of Lake Mariut where the water narrows to a thin finger. There we were seated comfortably, fifteen or twenty deep, along the sloping bank where both the north and south shores meet. It was not unlike an amphitheater, only the stage would be the lake itself. He then boarded a small boat and was rowed out upon the water a short distance and began to speak. To everyone's amazement, we could all hear him perfectly. His words sped unhindered across the calm waters of the lake. It was as if he were standing right next to us. He spoke for over three hours and never had to raise his voice."

"The Sea of Galilee!" Lazar's face beamed with pride at his prophetic powers.

"Of course!" Brother Apollonius agreed.

Clopas seemed lost for a moment but then looked up and giggled madly. "Oh! My boy, my boy, you *are* inspired. Do you know how inspired you are? Of course you do! Of course you do! Listen to me! Our myths tell us Noah saved our fathers from the great flood; Moses was drawn from the waters of the Nile and delivered us at the Red Sea. All our saviors issue from the water. Look how the followers of John responded to your appearance at the baptismal pool!"

"I'm sure you are correct, Uncle, but I was only thinking of the practicality of—"

Clopas jumped to his feet and threw his blanket to the floor. "It is much more than practical! Listen to me! Before you utter a word, my boy, you will paint a picture—the vision of a king emerging like a spirit out of the water. I assure you, my friends, it will penetrate the innermost chamber of our unremembered dreams, like Oannes the fish-man—the god who brought civilization to the ancient Chaldeans and thence to all our race. The story of Jonah stepping out of a great fish to enlighten the Ninevites is just the Hebrew variation of that old tale, you know."

Clopas's discourses on esoteric subjects could last hours. Jesus caught the eye of Brother Apollonius, and they shared a sigh of resigned sufferance.

"Don't you two smile at me like that! Yes, I said a *fish-man*—a god in the form of a fish-man—walked right out of the river in Babylon and forced our ancestors to listen to him—gave them the alphabet, gave them laws, taught them the secrets of the seasons and planting, put an end to cannibalism and bestiality..."

Lazar couldn't suppress a giggle. "But sir, with all due respect, you surely do not believe such a wonder actually occurred."

"Of course it did not *occur*," Clopas barked. "But *something* happened—something very profound happened, and whatever that something was gave birth to the myth, and myths are greater than history. Myths last forever. Myths change the world."

"But a fish-savior?" teased Lazar. "I'm afraid our simple Galilean neighbors do not possess your vast knowledge of regional mythology. I cannot recall a fish-god stepping out of the waters of my dreams."

"Look into the waters of the Dead Sea, young man," Clopas interrupted. "Darkness obscures your vision within a few inches, yet in places its depth cannot be fathomed. Mark my words. When your master appears upon the water, preaching his wisdom and hope to these poor wretches, he will be casting his net into the deepest abyss of the Jewish soul. No, no, no, my friends, this will not be the image of a mere wonder-worker. This is not the vision of a political provocateur. This will be the specter of a god-man, a savior king—a *Messiah*—and every drop of Semitic blood will quietly awaken and remember."

Clopas fell silent for a moment and caught his breath. He picked up his blanket and returned to his seat near the oven and turned his face toward Jesus. "And without having to make one pronouncement that might be judged seditious, without preaching one sermon deemed heretical by the Pharisees, your image will brand the memories of all who see you upon the water."

"I think we all agree it is a good idea, my lord," said Brother Apollonius. "So let us now discuss logistics." Taking a handful of flour from a nearby bin, he dusted the kneading board. With his finger he drew a harp-shaped oval representing the Sea of Galilee. Then, poking his finger here and there around the perimeter, he marked out cities. "Magdala, Capernaum, Chorazin, Bethsaida, Gergesa, Gamala, Sinnabris, Hammath, Tiberias, Dalmanutha."

Jesus stared intently at the map. "I will speak first at the synagogue at Capernaum. The hazzan there is our confederate. If all goes well, I will speak upon the water later that same day. Then, if it is possible, I will stay a day at Bethsaida, then move on to Gergesa, then Gamala. At Sinnabris the beloved disciples can baptize at the Jordan, then Hammath and Rakkath, and then finally at Magdala. If the crowds permit, I can walk part of the way; if not, I can hire a boat and sail from town to town."

Lazar interrupted, "Master, what about the pupils here at Cana? Are we to herd them all like sheep around the sea?"

"Why not?" answered Brother Apollonius. "They will serve as the sympathetic and enthusiastic core of every assembly. Besides, some of them hail from the very places we will be visiting. Their knowledge of local matters may prove invaluable."

"Also, my friends, also..." Clopas jumped to his feet and became so excited he could hardly get his words out. "Listen to me! Let each pupil carry, inconspicuously of course, bread, dried fruit, and salted fish to share with the hungry multitude who most certainly—most certainly, indeed—will have missed a meal or two to hear our 'savior.' What a heavenly treat! Fill their souls and fill their stomachs. 'This is a king who truly delivers,' they will say."

"Uncle, I am not sure—"

"Listen to me! I will arrange for boats to carry additional provisions to secretly resupply our flock near Gergesa, Gamala, and Tarichaea. Just send an angel to tell me when you will be there. We will actually fatten the flock. It will appear miraculous—miraculous!"

Brother Apollonius leaned over and placed his hand upon Clopas's knee to politely calm his enthusiasm. In the moment of silence, he turned to Jesus. "Medical wonders must also now begin in earnest, my friend. After the wedding miracle, the hearts of these Galileans will be rich in self-healing trust, and you must be prepared to tap and direct that great power before it dissipates."

Jesus raised his hand in protest. "I do not have to be reminded of the healing power of faith, but you know I lack the physical stature and the dramatic skills to bewitch the minds of so many at once."

"Then you must learn them or perish! Many years ago in Nubia I witnessed a great explosion of healings and wonders that manifested through the personality of one unassuming little man who was prone to fits of falling down and barking. When the fits subsided, his personality transformed for a short time into that of a local deity. His family discovered that when the deity was upon the fellow, he could heal with the touch of his hands. Naturally, word spread, and soon the entire village became vigilant to the sound of his barking and rushed to be near him.

"The healings themselves were nothing short of miraculous, but the greatest wonder was how the entire village was affected. Confident in the knowledge that the healing deity would soon dwell among them, the bodies and minds of the villagers proceeded to cry out to be healed of *hidden* maladies. Poisons that infected the blood and organs leached to the surface of the skin as boils and sores. Half the village appeared leprous. Diseases of the mind also surfaced as demon possession. Of course, once in the presence of the deity, the boils drained and the demons fled. It was really quite remarkable.

"Believe me, in the pandemonium of the days to come, you will heal countless patients who were not even ill before they heard you were coming. This sight will bolster the self-healing power of the seriously afflicted. For a short time at least, I am afraid you have no choice but to accept your new power to heal the masses. Play your part and be grateful that you can bring relief to their suffering."

"And after Galilee?" Jesus ran his finger around the edge of the sea on the flour map. "All this is well and good while we skirt the shore of the sea, but we cannot limit the ministry to Galilee. Eventually we must move south to Judaea, where the land swarms with informers and the Pharisees will dissect our every word. We cannot be caught feeding the multitudes with sleight of hand or traipsing about with a troop of naive pupils and Carmelite monks disguised as believers."

"But you will need some kind of protection," growled Clopas. "The council will never allow you to travel alone to Judaea."

Lazar moved to the kneading board. "Master, what if after your sermons by the sea the pupils and most of the beloved disciples return quietly to Cana and you travel south accompanied by a handful of your new Galilean followers?"

"Preposterous!" Clopas snapped.

Jesus smiled and looked at Lazar with great interest. "Let us hear the boy out, Uncle. Proceed, Lazar."

"As we move around the sea, it will be inevitable that many locals will elect to follow you. Choose from among them common men, men who are strong but who have never labored in their minds. Bid them walk by your side so that the multitude will know of your love for such as them. Invite them to travel with you to Judaea. Inspire them with your piety and wisdom. Instruct them with Essene parables. Heal them. But for their safety and your own, keep your new Galilean entourage oblivious of the Plan. Their ignorance will serve as a shield against the guile of our enemies and render them incapable of inadvertently betraying you. Can you imagine the bewilderment of the Scribes and Pharisees when they see you surrounded by a band of northern bumpkins?"

"It is true. You would not appear to be much of a threat to Rome either," Brother Apollonius agreed.

"'Your disciples will be idiots, and those that love you will be more dangerous than your enemies.'" Jesus remembered out loud the words of the abbot.

Mary's kitchen fell silent.

"The lad's a genius," Clopas whispered.

CHAPTER TWO

Then his disciples drew near to him and said, Why do you speak to them in parables? He answered, saying to them, Because to you it is granted to know the mystery of the kingdom of heaven, but it is not granted to them.

—*Matthew 13:10–11*

At daybreak, Clopas slipped away from the compound and set out by ass to Magdala to arrange for the supplies to feed the multitudes and the boats to deliver them.

"You have my proxy if the council should convene before my return," he shouted to Jesus as he trotted his ass through the gate.

In the days that followed, life at the Cana compound was chaos. The beloved disciples busied themselves making arrangements for the "walk on the water" (as they dubbed the Galilean campaign). At the same time, they tried desperately to cope with the influx of new pupils arriving each day, drawn by news of the wedding miracle. Jesus used the time to organize his thoughts concerning the content and character of the sermons he would deliver.

He barricaded himself in his chamber and rehearsed in his mind the classic lectures of Essene wisdom. His favorites were the beatitudes and Syrian parables. However, his real challenge would be to announce his coming kingdom without committing an act of sedition or blasphemy.

Public speaking was a dangerous affair in Roman Palestine. John had paid with his life. For over two generations, the only way a man of conviction could speak his mind publicly was to speak in innuendos and allegories. The people seemed to enjoy the game. Even the most unsophisticated citizen could read between the lines of a well-crafted parable, and the expert spinner of such yarns took pride in being able to embody multiple levels of meaning in the most inane-sounding tale.

Jesus's message was the most dangerous a man could deliver in public: revolution—the overthrow of the established Herodian government, long maintained by conspiracy and force. Because his burgeoning fame was the result of his persona as miracle-working holy man and healer, it followed that he must veil this message in religious and scriptural allusions. But in doing so he would simultaneously open himself to the scrutiny of the religious institutions, some of which, like the Pharisees, could brand him a blasphemer and heretic and have him put to death for the most innocuous breach of their interpretation of Mosaic law. It was a dangerously thin line to walk, and he knew he would have to push the limits on both fronts.

Seven days before Jesus was to depart for his walk upon the water, Joseph of Ramtha arrived at the compound alone and unannounced. He was ushered to Jesus's chamber.

"I have heard from Perez Ben Elam that you will soon begin to fatten the flock on the shores of Lake Tiberias. Do you plan to turn the sea to wine?"

"No, but Uncle Clopas has reckoned how to fill the stomachs of the multitudes with miraculous bread and fish."

Joseph placed a scroll of the book of Isaiah upon the little table near the window.

"The Sea of Galilee. You have chosen your first venue wisely." He unrolled the scroll to a marked passage and read aloud. "'In the past he humbled the land of Zebulun and the land of Naphtali, but in the future he will honor Galilee of the Gentiles, by the way of the sea, along the Jordan.' Have you given much thought to the content of your public message?"

"I have thought of little else since the marriage feast."

"I hope you will allow me to join your deliberations. I am an old survivor and not without skill in crafting language that says one thing and means another. Where can I get a clean scroll and a pot of ink?"

Jesus produced the items and shouted downstairs for food and drink.

The two talked through the night. By daybreak, they had crystallized their thoughts around a central theme. Jesus would further advance the message of John the Baptist and preach of the coming theocracy as a subjective spiritual utopia, which he would refer to as the "kingdom of heaven." To ensure that the population knew that the *kingdom of heaven* was to be the restoration of the mythical kingdom of David, he would make constant reference to the *Father in heaven*. Furthermore, he would declare his royal birthright by referring to himself as the *Son of the Father*.

Of course, the concept of God as a father was foreign to the Jewish mind. At the very least, it was shockingly revolutionary, and Jesus and Joseph debated for hours the wisdom of conjuring this new and potentially heretical image of deity. *Abraham* was the father of the Jews and father figure *to* the Jews. Abraham never referred to God as "Father"; neither did Moses, nor Elijah. In fact, in all the scriptures, only two verses in the book of Isaiah and one psalm of David made such allusions. Still, they agreed that these scraps of text could be cited, if necessary, to assuage any criticism that Jesus was introducing a new god to the children of Israel. The fact that Jesus could prove his direct hereditary descent from fathers Abraham, David, and Saul made it an irresistible and key element to the parable of his "Sonship" in the "kingdom of heaven."

"At no time must you or your followers be tricked into saying that the Father is God or that you are the Son of God," Joseph whispered, as if spies were in the room. "That would be the death of us all. Take shelter in vagueness. I assure you, those with ears to hear will immediately know what you are saying." Joseph yawned as he stood up and stretched his arms in the warmth of the dawning sunlight. "And those without ears to hear will simply see a healer—a handsome holy man to hail and follow. And now, my lord, I drowse. Tell me where I can nap. The Council of Seven meets here at high noon."

This news caught Jesus by surprise. "Uncle Clopas has embarked for Magdala, but I hold his proxy. You may sleep here; I will rest for a while in the library."

As he reached the stairs, Joseph of Ramtha called after him. "Oh, please inform that young spy for the abbot of Carmel and your mentor, the master physician, that the council craves their presence at the noon meeting."

Jesus did not like the sound of those words. He nodded his acknowledgment.

After relaying Joseph's ominous message to Lazar and Brother Apollonius, Jesus returned to the library and stretched out upon the floor to rest. He tried to sleep but could not.

CHAPTER THREE

And he sent two of his disciples, and said to them, Go to the city, and behold you will meet a man carrying a vessel of water; follow him. And wherever he enters, say to the owner of the house, Our master says, Where is the guestchamber where I may eat the passover with my disciples? And he will show you a large upper room furnished and prepared; there make ready for us.

—*Mark 14:13–15*

The Council of Seven assembled in the library. The spacious room afforded little relief from the midday heat. The conspirators stripped to the waist and sat in the shadows along two walls and bickered like cronies at a Roman bath.

"Where is Clopas? He has allowed the Plan to career out of control."

"It had to start sometime, somewhere. You have plotted safely in your mind for thirty years. Now you have no stomach when we begin in earnest?"

"How dare you question my heart or my stomach for violence! My Zealators have slain a score of nobles and bureaucrats who would hinder our Lord's ascension. But many more must be liquidated before the way is cleared for our savior's triumphal entry into Jerusalem. Barabbas estimates two more years of—"

"My lords, please!" Joseph of Ramtha rose from his seat and gestured for Lazar to close the shutters to the courtyard. "No one is suggesting that we are ready to purchase the ass for our Messiah's trot into the city."

Lazar giggled as if he expected laughter from the entire assembly. None came.

Joseph of Ramtha cleared his throat and continued, "One thing is clear, however: the great drama has begun, and we must accept the opening act and amend the plot accordingly. Do not worry, my friend; I think we can buy a year or two more for our band of Zealators to finish weeding the garden."

This time the council members chuckled slyly. Lazar remained silent.

"In the meantime, the good word of the coming kingdom will be preached by Jesus the Nazarite, a holy man from Galilee, who turns water into wine, heals the sick, and feeds the hungry—and who, by the time the garden is weeded, will be the most famous man in all of Roman Palestine."

The council listened all afternoon as Joseph and Jesus revealed the allegorical subtleties of the kingdom of heaven. All agreed that the message was masterfully crafted and discussed how best to arrange for provocateurs to follow in the wake of Jesus's travels to clarify the word among the most radical and motivated elements in each community.

Brother Apollonius and Lazar outlined the details of the coming walk on the water and the feeding of the multitudes. Everyone agreed it was a brilliant idea, and Elam of Japhia, who owned property in the north, offered to stock the caves between Tyre and Sidon should Jesus bring his message closer to the coast.

However, the council was not of one mind concerning Lazar's idea of Jesus traveling with a retinue of Galilean brutes. Although they all eventually conceded the basic wisdom of the Plan, there was much debate over how Jesus and the council could stay in communication under such circumstances.

Joseph of Ramtha listened quietly to the arguments. Finally, he stood to speak. "My friends, we have listened all afternoon to the wise counsel of Brother Apollonius and young Lazar. I'm sure it will not surprise any of you to learn that they both are agents of the abbot of the monastery of Mount Carmel. As one of our oldest and dearest supporters, the abbot has seen to the education of our king-to-be and has supplied us the beloved disciples who shepherd the pupils of our mass movement. Is there any among us who doubts the abbot's fidelity or the goodwill and loyalty of Brother Apollonius and Lazar?"

With only one exception, the elders voiced their support. Ephron of Arbela abstained and asked for the floor.

"My lords, while I certainly have no reservations concerning the fealty of the good abbot or the good intentions of Brother Apollonius and Lazar, I confess that I harbor some doubts about young Lazar. Not only is he very young, but I question whether or not the fire of racial passion burns hot enough in his veins."

"What are you taking about?" Jesus jumped to his feet. "Lazar is—"

"A Canaanite Samaritan!" Ephron calmly interrupted. Jesus fell silent and turned to Lazar, then to Joseph of Ramtha.

Lazar cleared his throat. "My lords, may I speak?"

"Of course, my son," Joseph said.

"It is true. I am a Samaritan, the son of a Canaanite whore. My father was a goldsmith—an observant Judaean Jew. He also fathered my two older sisters. He bore great love for my mother and upon his death provided generously for her and her children. As I was the only male child he ever sired, he bequeathed me his home in Bethany with instructions that my mother and two sisters be allowed to live there. However, he had other plans for me. After my mother and sisters were settled in Bethany, I was taken to the Essene monastery on Mount Carmel and there enrolled for instruction. I was six years old. I am now sixteen and have only returned home once in that time—four years ago to visit my sisters when my mother died.

"Please, my lords, in my heart I am every bit as much of an Essene Jew as Brother Apollonius or my master or any of the beloved disciples. Do not make my blood stand against me as witness. I have been baptized. I am circumcised. I pleaded with the abbot to allow me to leave the monastery and serve the master. I have been with the movement since Jericho. More than anything on earth, I desire to continue and help bring the great plan to fruition."

"And since you arrived at Cana you have been the abbot's angel—carrying regular reports to Carmel; is this not true?" Joseph of Ramtha asked.

"Yes, my lord—with the full knowledge of yourself and the entire council."

"These messages, do you inscribe them on parchment or relay them through other messengers?"

"Indeed *not*, sir! I deliver all messages personally; for security I rely entirely upon my memory. I am blessed with an extraordinary memory, a talent that earned me my situation as the abbot's valet. Sir, I had no idea that my duties were viewed with suspicion. The abbot is a principal of the movement; he trusts my fealty and discretion."

"And so do we," Joseph said with a smile. "Do we not, my lords?"

The council, including Ephron of Arbela, nodded and mumbled their unanimity.

Jesus marveled at the skill with which Joseph of Ramtha had manipulated the council. With only token debate he unilaterally drafted Brother Apollonius and young Lazar as key players in an elite conspiracy that spanned three generations.

"Gentlemen!" Joseph's manner turned coldly businesslike. "Lazar's idea is sound, and I urge that we follow his suggestion. Our savior should be insulated as long as possible by a thick membrane of common folk and simpletons. However, it would be folly for *us* to leave him completely to the canaille, so I am suggesting that Brother Apollonius and Lazar also remain part of his entourage."

"But what about his safety? The council cannot be isolated from his movements or the day-to-day difficulties that may arise," said Elam of Japhia.

"Our king will never be more than half a day away from the shadow of our wings. Here is my plan. We will post a string of confederates, one in every village, town, and city along his route. They will stand ready to see to his needs as he passes and relay messages between Jesus and the council.

"Lazar will be our angel and carry the names and locations of each agent in his talented head and will run ahead each day with news of the troop's approach and return with pertinent information."

The council was impressed. Elam was particularly enchanted with the idea. He turned to Jesus and smiled. "It will further add to your reputation for omniscience."

"If I were omniscient, I would know what you are talking about," Jesus laughed. "Please explain."

"Let us imagine that you wish to dine with your band of Galileans in a certain town you are approaching. Send Lazar quietly ahead to instruct our agent stationed there to arrange for a room and a sumptuous meal. Lazar will then return and secretly inform you that the feast will be waiting and that a man carrying a pitcher of water or a man with an eye patch or a wooden leg will lead you there. You then, with great and mystic solemnity, instruct two or three of your followers, 'Go now into the city and look for a man with an eye patch. Say to him, "My master asks: Where is my guest room where I may eat my supper with my disciples?'" Without a word, the mysterious one-eyed man will lead them to the feasting hall and tell them, 'The master's supper awaits!'"

The entire council broke into laughter. Everyone talking at once, they each added their own comic hypothetical variation. It was a lighthearted moment and a pleasant conclusion to the day's deliberations.

It was early evening when the meeting adjourned with everyone in high spirits. Lazar departed immediately to Carmel to update the abbot and receive permission to escalate his duties. Jesus and Brother Apollonius convened the beloved disciples and briefed them on the new phase of the program. To everyone's delight, four of them hailed from the very towns and villages Jesus was about to pass through on his way south to Judaea. All eagerly volunteered to be posted in their hometowns. Brother Matthias, the son of a wealthy merchant in Jerusalem, begged to be stationed in the Holy City to coordinate housing and security for the eventual triumphal entry. The Plan was taking on a life of its own; everyone could feel the momentum.

By the time Lazar returned from Carmel two days later, the list of agents was ready for him to memorize. Nothing now remained but to choose the beloved disciples and pupils for the walk upon the water.

CHAPTER FOUR

As he walked beside the sea of Galilee, he saw Simon and Andrew his brother throwing their nets into the sea; for they were fishermen. And Jesus said to them, Follow me and I will make you fishers of men.

—Mark 1:16–17

Calib pulled his net into the boat and spit into the sea. He had been fishing with Simon and Andrew for only two days and already his coarse manners and body odor were becoming intolerable. "Andrew, did you hear that your master, John the Baptizer, lost his head at Sepphoris?"

It was clearly the wrong thing to say to Andrew.

"Of course he heard, you Gadarene swine!" The small boat rocked violently as Andrew's brother Simon rose up and threatened to throw Calib into the sea. "If you want to keep fishing for Zebedee, you will keep your filthy mouth shut."

"I deserted him at Aenon," Andrew sobbed quietly, not looking up from his net. "I should have remained at his side or followed the son of Joseph the Great Carpenter. My master called him the 'Lamb of God.' I did not understand his words. He spoke them so strangely. What did he mean? What did he mean?"

"I suppose your master saw something in the Nazarite," Simon answered as he stared at the horizon. "Is he not the same who turned water to wine at the wedding of Isaac Ben Samuel in Cana?"

"Perhaps," Andrew sighed. "Perhaps we are all Lambs of God—just living to be slaughtered."

"His pupils also baptize." Simon tried to lighten the conversation. "I have heard how he healed the afflicted as he walked from Nazareth to Cana. If he were here, I would take him to heal Hannah's mother."

"Hannah's mother will soon be gathered unto our fathers," Andrew mumbled as he untangled his net and prepared to cast. "Would I were sleeping in the bosom of Abraham."

Andrew and Simon were sons of Jonah the boat builder of Bethsaida. Since they were children, they had labored for the family of Zebedee, the prosperous master of a flotilla of fishing vessels on the Sea of Galilee and the father of their boyhood friends, James and John. When the boys were very young, they performed the loathsome chores around the gutting tables, but as they grew older, their duties moved them to the salting sheds. Here they were made privy to the subtle secrets that made Zebedee's dried fish a prized essential for well-set tables from Caesarea to Jericho. This day, at the request of Simon's father-in-law, they fished near Capernaum, the home of Simon's espoused, Hannah, whose mother lay gravely ill.

Simon was a huge man with thick red hair and a beard that masked his mouth and ears. Not yet twenty-one, his manner and girth made him the very image of Goliath. He was slow-witted and never mastered the written word, but his heart was tender, and his simple honesty touched his family and employer. Because of Simon's girth and fearsome countenance, Zebedee charged him with the responsibility of traveling each month up to Jerusalem to deliver fish to the household of a most important customer, Caiaphas, the high priest of the Temple. Caiaphas's monthly order was substantial and the road to his palace beset by thieves. Simon's titanic stature was an effective deterrent to those who might be tempted to relieve him of his payment on his journey home.

Andrew was two years younger than Simon. Since childhood he was drawn to all things spiritual, but like his brother Simon, he was deemed too dull of wit to be formally educated. He frequented the synagogue and listened intently to the words of the rabbi and other learned men but found he could not follow their rhetoric. He made regular pilgrimages up to Jerusalem, where he sat outside the Temple for hours and listened to the ravings of would-be prophets who babbled from dawn to dusk on the Temple steps.

It was there that he first heard of John the Nazarite. He went immediately to the Jordan and was baptized. John was everything Andrew was seeking. John understood everything. John was not confused. John knew exactly what to believe. When the Baptizer grabbed Andrew by the hair and leaned him back into the muddy waters, a lifetime of fear and frustration dissolved from his soul. When he resurfaced, he realized he would never have to understand the scriptures—he would never have to understand the law. To know the mind of God, he need only believe in John.

He did not understand the earthly forces that moved against his master or the reasons for his arrest and execution. Now that John was dead, Andrew's despair was profound. Only the awkward love of his brother Simon and his old playmates, James and John, prevented him from taking his own life.

"What is happening on the shore?" Simon asked quietly, as if talking to himself. "There must be a hundred people following that man."

"It's probably the wine-making magician from Cana," smirked Calib. "The hazzan has invited him to speak in the synagogue."

Andrew stood up and shaded his eyes with his hands. "Simon, please. Row us closer to the shore."

"But what about our catch?" Calib whined. "At this hour no schools swim near the shore."

"Shut up, fool!" Simon snarled.

As they drew nearer the shore and the approaching procession, Andrew spied the leader of the throng. "Simon! Simon! It is he! It is he whom my master called the Lamb of God!"

———

Jesus pulled Brother Apollonius close to his side and whispered, "Have we secured a boat for tomorrow's sermon?"

"I will see to it this afternoon while you speak at the synagogue. Boats are everywhere. One like that will be ideal for our purpose." He pointed toward the sea to a fishing boat drawing near the shore.

"Wait, I know that man!" Jesus stopped and grabbed Brother Apollonius by the arm and pointed at Andrew. "He is a disciple of John. I saw him at my baptism."

Brother Apollonius squinted to get a better look. "Do you see the size of the red-beard beside him? If you had a Goliath like that by your side the council would never need fear for your safety."

———

"Andrew, look. The holy man points at you—at *you*!"

"*Ewe*! Of course! Ewe! The *Lamb* points at *ewe*; it thinks *ewe* are its mother!" Poor Calib's joke was ill-timed. His snigger turned to shrieks of terror as Simon grabbed him by the hair and hurled him overboard into the sea. The splash turned the heads of all walking at the water's edge. Forgetting the insult, Andrew grabbed his net and threw it overboard as a lifeline. Preferring to take his chances with the sea rather than return to the boat, Calib dog-paddled the short distance to the beach. Everyone on shore was laughing because, to all appearances, Simon and Andrew were trying to use their nets to catch Calib like a fish.

Jesus called for Lazar. "Quickly, see if any among us know these fishermen."

Almost immediately Lazar returned with a young pupil. "Master, they are Simon and Andrew, the sons of Jonah from Bethsaida. They work for the house of Zebedee. All of Judaea eats his salted fish."

Jesus broke from the crowd and waded ankle-deep into the sea toward the boat. "Simon! Andrew! What are you doing?"

The brothers were paralyzed. "He hails us by name," Andrew whispered.

"Shall we answer him?"

"What do we say?"

"He asks what we are doing."

"He asks what we are *doing*?"

"Yes. He said, 'Simon and Andrew, what are you doing?'"

"What *are* we doing?"

"Fishing. We are fishing!"

"Tell him, then. Tell him we are fishing."

"You tell him."

"That we are fishing?"

"Yes!"

Andrew cleared his throat. Cupping his hands around his mouth, he yelled, "Fishing, my lord!"

At that moment, a few yards down the beach, Calib dragged himself out of the water and collapsed on the sand.

Jesus giggled. "I see you have let a big one get away!"

The brothers could not think of a reply.

"Come, Simon and Andrew! Follow me, and I will make you fishers of men."

CHAPTER FIVE

Jesus travelled throughout Galilee, teaching in their synagogues and preaching the good news of the kingdom, and healing every kind of disease and sickness among the people.

—*Matthew 4:23*

"What do you want with us, Nazarite? Have you come to destroy us? I know who you are—the Holy One of God!"

Jesus expected something like this. Not halfway through his sermon, a demon-possessed man interrupted his first synagogue discourse. He had no choice but to perform an exorcism then and there.

"Be silent!" Jesus ordered in a voice that terrified everyone in the room. He could not allow every demon he exorcised to define his title of authority; otherwise, he would soon be reduced to the role of a magician—casting out in the name of Belial or Beelzebub.

"Be silent! Silent! Devil! You will come out of him now! I command you!" Jesus had done this scores of times.

The man let out a shriek and fell to the floor in the very center of the congregation. He shook violently and soiled himself. Suddenly he fell silent. He stopped shaking and lay motionless on the floor. He appeared dead.

"Get up!" Jesus shouted. "Get up!"

The man immediately regained consciousness and loudly sucked in his breath as if it were his first breath as a baby. He returned to his feet and looked around as if he were unsure where he was. "I am delivered! Lord, I am delivered!" His face beamed with joy and relief. "The teacher has delivered me!"

The congregation was amazed. "What is this? What authority! He even gives orders to evil spirits, and they obey him. This Nazarite speaks with the voice of the Almighty."

Seeing this wonder, Simon pushed his way to Jesus and knelt before him. "Master, please, Milcah, the mother of my espoused wife, lies near death at her home not far from here. Let us take you there so you might make her whole."

Jesus quietly answered, "Lead me to her."

The synagogue emptied as the entire congregation followed Jesus, Simon, and Andrew down the street to the home of Simon's in-laws. Children ran ahead of the throng and alerted the household of the approach of the healing holy man.

"Milcah, awake! Simon comes with the holy man, Jesus, the son of Mary the widow of Joseph the Great Carpenter. He comes to heal you of your fever!"

"Oh, dear God!" Milcah lifted her fevered head from her pillow and surveyed her surroundings. "Look at my house. All of Capernaum will see it like this. Simon does not have a brain in his thick head."

She sat up in bed for the first time in three days and reached for her robe. "Somebody! Get this chamber pot out of here! Bring me a wet cloth for my face. What is stinking in the kitchen? Throw it out! Lay out bread and salt! And cheese! Cheese! And wine! Fetch wine! If we have none, go to the neighbors and beg some! Will someone bring me something to cover my head? Did you hear me? Get this stinking chamber pot out of here!"

"Lie back down, my dear; you are too weak to—"

"Husband, be still! I have strength enough not to die with my house looking like this!"

"My dear, please lie down. They are already here."

"Anna! Anna! Tell Anna to greet the holy man and wash his feet. Purchase me time to tidy this chamber! His family owns half of Galilee!"

Jesus could not refuse the kind gesture of a foot washing and perceived that his presence had already evoked the healing spirit of a homemaker's pride. He stopped the young man who was removing the chamber pot. He glanced inside and lightly sniffed the contents. "Food poisoning," he silently diagnosed. "She will recover if her will to live prevails."

Finally, Simon was allowed to take Jesus to Milcah's bedchamber. The hazzan and a dozen men from the synagogue stood near and peered through the door. Simon timidly made the introductions.

"Mother, this is my master. He has come to make you well."

"Simon, you have deceived me," Jesus said warmly. "Where is the mother of your wife? I see only this lovely maiden."

Although she knew he was teasing her, the old woman swooned, "Oh, my lord, you are too kind." She sat up and squirmed coquettishly against her pillows.

Jesus approached her bed and sat down. He placed his palm on her forehead. His hand was cool and brought her instant relief. She closed her eyes and took a deep breath. He gently took her hand.

"Come, good woman. The fever has departed your house. See? It has been replaced by guests who love you." Jesus raised her by the hand and led her through the onlookers and into her kitchen. With the help of young Hannah, she helped prepare and serve the evening meal to Jesus, Simon, and Andrew.

Before they had finished their meal, they were interrupted by a commotion taking place in the street in front of the house. Jesus opened the door and beheld an apocalyptic scene. As far as he could see down both sides, the street was jammed with broken humanity: the afflicted and the demon-possessed. The cacophony was deafening. The possessed barked and howled and crowed like roosters. They tore at their garments and spat obscenities and blasphemies. The sick moaned and lamented of their afflictions, and relatives and friends pleaded on their behalf.

Jesus called for Brother Apollonius and Lazar, who were resting inside the house. He instructed Lazar to run to the shore and bring the most experienced of the beloved disciples to provide order and security. He didn't have to speak to Brother Apollonius, who immediately waded into the horde and began to survey the situation and determine how best to form the queue of afflicted.

Jesus worked through the night, healing them one by one. He started with the cases of obvious hypochondria. With each success, the onlookers exploded in a chorus of thunderous praise. By the time he reached the seriously ill, the power of their faith was so strong that Jesus need only touch them and declare them healed.

It was almost dawn when two young men approached carrying a man on a litter.

"He eats, my lord, constantly with a ravenous hunger. Yet he is never satisfied—and his body wastes to bones."

Jesus pulled back the blanket that covered the man and beheld a living skeleton. He marveled that the breath of life could still inhabit so frail a scaffolding. Set deep in the pits of a hollow skull, two black eyes stared up with a helpless prayer. He placed his hands on the poor man's abdominal cavity and gently probed to feel the condition of the internal organs.

"Where is this man from?"

"From Gadara, my lord. He is a swineherd."

The pious Jews in the crowd backed away. The man was unclean.

"Jesus, son of David, you...can heal me...if you want to," the skeleton spoke through slits of lips that never closed.

"I want to," Jesus whispered.

He ordered Simon to fill a clay pot with the coals from the communal oven. He then called for a skin of soured milk. There was none in the house of Milcah, so pupils were dispatched to awaken the neighboring households. In a few minutes, a young man returned with a bloated skin that leaked a stinking pus of spoiled goat's milk.

Jesus instructed Simon to fetch the jar of coals and bring it to the side of the dying man's litter. Jesus took the skin of milk and squeezed a putrid stream into the gaping mouth of the skeleton, who immediately choked and spit out the horrible brew. Jesus squirted another dose of stinking curds straight down the old man's throat.

Next, he poured a generous amount into the jar of coals. It hissed and steamed upon the blazing embers. The smell was horrific. Onlookers gagged and covered their faces as they backed far away from the nauseating fumes. Jesus helped the man to sit up and held his head directly over the stinking pot.

"Breathe."

"Oh, dear lord, no!" The poor man struggled, but Jesus held his face to the rising vapors.

"Breathe!" he commanded.

He coughed and gagged. "Please, my lord...no!"

"Breathe!" Jesus bellowed. "Choke the wicked spirit! Breathe, I say! Vomit! Vomit! Spew it out!"

"But my belly...is...is empty, lord!" the poor man pleaded between gasps.

"Lies! Lies! It is filled with the unclean demon of filth! Come out of him! Come out of him!"

The man could no longer struggle; he heaved and coughed and retched a bloody paste into the mouth of the horrible pot, causing a new cloud of foul steam to rise into his nostrils. He was choking to death. Witnesses turned their heads in pity and disgust. Lazar had never seen anything like this.

"Has he lost his mind? He will kill that poor devil," he whispered to Brother Apollonius. "We've got to stop this!"

"Do not interfere. Watch. I taught him this."

Lazar ignored the warning. He covered his face with the neck of his garment and ran to the side of the litter. He put his hands on the man's bony shoulders and tried to drag him away from the suffocating vapor. Jesus did nothing to stop him. The coughing had ceased. The man could no longer breathe. Jesus released his grip and slowly backed away. He locked his eyes upon the terrified face of his bewildered patient. The man rotated his quivering head and looked helplessly at Lazar. The sight was terrifying. The red and dripping skin barely concealed the sutures of his skull. His jaw wagged low, and he struggled to make a sound. Lazar could not take his eyes away from the hideous face. From the black abyss of his toothless mouth, the skeleton's narrow tongue darted out like the head of a snake. It was thin and pale, and it wavered in the air just inches away from the lad's face. Then, to Lazar's horror, the obscene tongue shot forward and slapped him on the lips with its hot stinking slime. Lazar screamed and recoiled so violently that he fell flat on his back in the street.

Jesus jumped between Lazar and the skeleton and seized the slippery tongue with both hands and began to pull. "Out of him, devil! Out of him!"

Lazar, still wiping slime from his lips, scrambled to get out of the way. Brother Apollonius stepped forward and pinned the man to the ground. Jesus continued to pull, hand over hand, as the tongue fell to the dust in a hideous writhing coil. Jesus's robe was covered in blood and slime. By the time the tail of the monster came out of the swine-herd's throat, more than twenty feet of slimy worm lay squirming in the dirt.

The man finally caught his breath and began to cough again. Jesus picked up the monstrous worm and dropped it in the jar of coals. The vessel crackled and trembled and jumped in the dirt as if it were alive and in agony.

"Simon! Cast this in the fire."

He returned to his patient and embraced him. The poor man could only cling to him and sob.

"The demon is gone. You will eat again. You will eat again and be filled. But observe the law, my friend. Eat not the flesh of swine. Go and err no more."

CHAPTER SIX

After these things Joseph of Ramtha, who was a disciple of Jesus, but secretly because of fear of the Jews, besought Pilate that he might take away the body of Jesus. And Pilate granted him permission. So he came and took away the body of Jesus.

—*John 19:38.*

The sun had fallen behind the hill.

"I am the owner of this property! The bodies must be down before sunset." The voice was that of Joseph of Ramtha. He spoke loudly and with such bold authority that the Temple soldiers jumped to their feet. Surprised by the appearance of a member of the Sanhedrin, the mob at the base of the hill fell hushed and strained to hear what was happening above.

"The one in the middle is dead. His people are here to dispose of the body," he shouted, indicating with an exaggerated sweep of his hand the hastily quarried tomb about two hundred paces from the execution area.

"Roman law forbids burial of the crucified," protested the captain of the Temple guard. But then he saw standing behind Joseph a centurion and two Roman soldiers.

"Nevertheless, I carry Pilate's order that it be so."

"What about the other two? They still live!" argued the Temple guard captain, *trying to resurrect some semblance of his authority.*

The centurion finally spoke. "My men are here to break their legs. Step away and let them do their duty, or I'll have them break your legs first."

Joseph of Ramtha added, "It's nearly the ninth hour. Pilate has ordered this carrion removed before the start of the Great Sabbath."

———

The walk on water exceeded everyone's expectations. Word spread faster and farther than anyone could have predicted. By the time Jesus reached Gamala on the eastern shore of the sea, his congregation included throngs who had traveled from as far away as Jerusalem and Damascus. So great was the response to Jesus's Galilee ministry that he decided to postpone (for the time being) taking it south to Judaea.

"Why travel to Judaea if the Judaeans travel to me?"

In Bethsaida, Simon and Andrew introduced Jesus to James and John, the sons of Zebedee. Jesus could hardly believe his eyes. The two were both nearly as enormous as Simon. Jesus laughed and called them *Boanerges,* "Sons of Thunder." The four became Jesus's bodyguards and the core of his Galilean disciples, which soon swelled to a dozen.

The Council of Seven was especially pleased to learn that the "Sons of Thunder" were part of the entourage. Their father's wealth was well known throughout Palestine. The enemies of the movement would mistakenly assume that it was Zebedee's riches that sustained the ministry and overlook the trail of gold leading to the real conspirators.

After circling the Sea of Galilee, the troop traveled north. The masses received the good news of a coming kingdom more with curiosity than understanding, but the message was secondary to Jesus's presence as a miracle worker and healer. Elam of Japhia delivered the magic of loaves and fishes from the caves on his property near Tyre. It was the largest and most convincing of the miraculous mass feedings—the food appearing seemingly from nowhere. Even Simon and Andrew and the Sons of Thunder were deceived. Nevertheless, it was the last time Jesus would allow such a sleight-of-hand deception to be perpetrated.

The intense hysteria that accompanied Jesus's acts of healing was unprecedented. Even Brother Apollonius admitted that he had never encountered anything like it. Sick people who had never laid eyes on Jesus found themselves healed after simply touching objects that they believed Jesus had touched. Provincial physicians and amateur magicians throughout the country began using the name "Jesus" to successfully heal and cast out evil spirits.

When Jesus learned of this, he decided to dispatch his disciples in all directions to heal in his name. Even the unskilled Galileans experienced a remarkable level of success. However, there was danger in this practice, for the Pharisees were ever vigilant, and the simple minds of the northern disciples were no match against them when challenged on points of the law. As it turned out, however, the employment of these surrogate healers proved a stroke of genius. The reputation of Jesus, the Galilean wonder-worker, was enhanced by every act done in his name. On any given day, miracles attributed to Jesus were said to occur simultaneously in five or six locations separated by a hundred miles or more. The Pharisees and those who sought to entrap him were never sure where he would appear next or even which of the dozens of wonder-workers was really Jesus.

The Council of Seven could not believe their good fortune. Joseph of Ramtha's prophecy was fulfilled. In just two years, Jesus had become the most famous man in Roman Palestine.

BOOK FOUR

WOMAN
OF THE WELL

CHAPTER ONE

So the soldiers came and broke the legs of the first, and of the other who was crucified with him. But when they came to Jesus, they saw that he was dead already, so they did not break his legs.

—*John 19:32–33*

The centurion directed his men to break the legs of the two condemned, who still showed signs of life. This grim duty was dispatched by wedging a large flat stone behind the ankle to force the knee forward, then clubbing the leg just below the knee with one mighty blow with a large setting maul. Crippled thusly, it would no longer be possible for the crucified to push themselves into position to breathe. They would suffocate to death within a few minutes.

When the first blow was delivered, the man cried out so loudly that Lazar feared Jesus would awaken or show signs of life. But Jesus did not awaken, nor did the pitiful cries of agony on his left and right stir him to movement of any kind.

———

The Galilean campaign lasted nearly two years. It was wildly successful, but the madness of his double life took its toll upon Jesus. As much as he was grateful for their protection and service, he grew increasingly impatient with the dullness of his Galilean disciples. He grew increasingly weary of keeping them ignorant of the great plan and the roles Lazar, Brother Apollonius, and the Carmelite beloved disciples were playing in the "ministry." More and more, Jesus seized every opportunity to remove himself from the company of the Galilean disciples. On three occasions, he slipped away from them and did not return for over a week.

One afternoon, Simon and Andrew returned from Caesarea Philippi to find Jesus suffering one of his increasingly frequent bouts of melancholy. He asked Simon, "Who do they say I am in the town?"

"Some say John the Baptist, others say Elijah, and still others, Jeremiah or one of the prophets," Simon answered cautiously.

"And Simon, who do you say I am?" Jesus asked sardonically.

"I say you are the anointed one, the Son of the living God."

This was precisely the dangerously foolish answer Jesus feared would fall from Simon's lips—precisely the type of interpretation of the message of the coming king that Joseph of Ramtha warned could lead to charges of blasphemy. Joseph was confident that even common men "who had ears to hear" would grasp Jesus's real meaning—that they would understand that the coming "kingdom" meant an end to Herod's rule and the establishment of a new Jewish kingdom here on earth, and at its helm would be a true "Son of the Father"—a prince of Davidian blood. Yet Joseph and the others (even Jesus himself) had not counted on the thick skulls of the twelve Galileans who now surrounded the "Messiah." They took the message at face value, for they could imagine nothing more. Jesus knew that if this simplistic understanding of his message should spread, it might precipitate just the kind of legalistic attack that could crush the Plan before it had a chance to succeed. He was also acutely aware that one wrong word could mean great personal danger for himself, the Council of Seven, and all their supporters. These innocent, loyal, honest Galileans who so revered him could actually be his undoing. "How could they be so dense?" he thought.

Jesus flew into a rage and called Simon a rock[11]—one of the most insulting epithets in the Aramaic language. Simon was crushed by his master's remark but even more humiliated when Jesus then launched into a diatribe of bitter frustration, sarcastically lamenting to the stunned Galilean disciples that the future kingdom would be built upon a foundation rock of such ignorance. He shook his finger at the frightened twelve and screamed that none of them should ever again refer to him as the "Son of God." Others who overheard the outburst became frightened. Some even decided to desert the movement.

On a return visit to Capernaum, Jesus suffered what Brother Apollonius diagnosed as a fatigue of the soul, a mental breakdown so severe that his mother, Mary, sent his brothers to bring him home for a rest. Jesus's brother James, who was growing ever more interested in the movement, even offered to lead the disciples while Jesus was away. Jesus would have none of it and sent them away with uncharacteristic rudeness.

Later he met privately with Lazar and Brother Apollonius and apologized for his behavior.

"You need a change, my friend," Brother Apollonius counseled. "Your brothers and their families are going up to Jerusalem to celebrate the Feast of Tabernacles. They send word they would like you to join them there."

"Absolutely not!" Jesus said. "How can I face them after the way I treated them—especially James?"

"The Sons of Thunder and a few of your followers and their families would also like to observe the feast in Jerusalem with you. If you

---

11. Aramaic, *Kepha*; Greek, *Petros*.

could abide their company for the journey, I am sure they would be honored and delighted to accompany you to the Temple."

"But don't you see, it is them I would escape! I cannot endure their idiotic chatter. They try my patience. Now they are telling everyone I'm the Son of God!"

"Perhaps you could ride ahead of them for part of the way. If you like, Lazar and I will secure mounts and join you. Let the Galileans tag along behind on foot. They will be as happy as children."

"Yes, master, please," Lazar agreed. "I should like to visit my sisters in Bethany. They know nothing of my adventures. They would be thrilled to see me. Also…" He cleared his throat and looked nervously at Brother Apollonius. "…also, I carry a message from the Council of Seven that it is time for you to cautiously make an appearance in Jerusalem. They realize there is danger, but they now wish to draw out and identify our enemies."

Brother Apollonius put his hands on the back of Jesus's shoulders and gently massaged the tension from his back and neck. "And if you are still in a sour mood, you can commit some provocative act at the Temple. *That* will give the council something to talk about."

The three laughed at the thought.

"Very well," Jesus sighed. "Tell the Rock and the Sons of Thunder that we will go up to Jerusalem. But let them know I am weary and will need to ride. You and Lazar will join me on mounts. We will talk. I will enjoy that. It will be like old times."

The three talked a while longer. Lazar mapped their route south through Samaria and Judaea and recited from memory the names and addresses of the agents stationed in the towns and villages through which they would pass.

The next morning, Lazar rode to Tiberias and alerted the beloved disciple residing there to relay word of the coming of the lord. He then went to the Cana estate to secure money for the journey. Mary filled a purse with far more silver than would be needed and begged Lazar to relay her love and concern. He returned two days later and found Jesus and the others ready to embark.

Among the pilgrims was Rhoda, the enormous mother of the Sons of Thunder. Moments before they set out for Jerusalem, she cornered Jesus and pushed her two sons down on their knees before him. She then struggled to her own knees and grabbed the front of Jesus's robe.

Trying not to appear irritated, he asked, "What is it you want?"

"Grant that one of these two sons of mine may sit at your right and the other at your left in your kingdom."

He did not know how to answer. In the last year, he had come to the realization that once he was king his world would change dramatically. These simple people had no idea to what extent they were being used. Their kind were likely to suffer most during the turmoil of establishing the new kingdom. He couldn't begin to tell her that her brutish sons would have no standing in a royal Davidian court, let alone a seat by his side. How could he even explain to this trembling woman that the kingdom for which he was preparing was an earthly affair, not the holy kingdom she imagined? He could not bring himself to lie to her, and so took refuge in the doublespeak of the message.

"Woman, you don't know what you are asking. To sit at my right hand and at my left, that is not mine to give; it is for those for whom it is prepared by my Father."

He broke her grasp and hurried to the mules, leaving the poor woman kneeling in the dust. The Sons of Thunder looked at each other with bewilderment. Simon, Andrew, and a handful of other followers overheard this exchange and, as soon as Jesus was out of sight, they attacked the brothers for their presumption. The quarrel was still raging as the procession set out for Jerusalem.

Jesus rode alone for the first few miles, leaving Lazar and Brother Apollonius trailing leisurely along behind the others.

"We must get his mind off his great responsibilities," whispered Brother Apollonius. "Whenever possible, engage him in conversation upon matters unrelated to the stresses of the kingdom."

"Such as what?" Lazar asked.

"You will think of something. He needs diversion."

Lazar thought for several moments, then urged his mule to the front of the train and joined his master. Brother Apollonius followed.

Jesus acknowledged the presence of his two friends and then turned to see why the disciples were making so much noise. "Lazar, what is going on back there?"

"Your army, my lord. They are arguing about which among them is your greatest disciple."

"Oh, how I tire of those idiots."

Jesus whipped his mule and trotted around a hill and out of sight of the pedestrians. Lazar and Brother Apollonius soon caught up.

Brother Apollonius caught Lazar's eye, signaling that he should initiate a pleasant diversion. Lazar acknowledged this with a confident wink and steered his mule nearer to Jesus's.

"Master, have you ever known a woman?"

Brother Apollonius couldn't believe his ears.

"Lazar! That will be quite enough!" He raised his whip and swatted the back of the young man's head. "That is not the kind of conversation I had in mind! It is inappropriate even for an Illuminated to question a Perfect Master on matters of such intimacy."

"Don't rebuke the lad," Jesus laughed. "He is a man now. We may speak as men. If we were still on the mountain, his class masters would answer such questions." Jesus was quiet for a moment, then tried to suppress a smile as he turned again to Lazar. "Why do you ask, my friend? Do you have unwed sisters?"

"Indeed, lord, I told you, Martha and Mary in Bethany. I haven't seen them in four years and..." Lazar suddenly realized he was being teased and flushed crimson. "Master, I was not suggesting..."

The three shared a hearty chuckle.

"Yes, Lazar. Aside from observing our order's routine calendar of purifications, I have taken no vows of sexual abstinence. As a boy of ten during my last year in Egypt, I was gently introduced to the mysteries of physical love by the doves of the Isisian guild. As an adult, I have known a number of women as a man knows his wife. If ever I should ascend the throne, you can be sure I shall be expected to breed an heir."

Lazar was visibly shocked. "But does not the law reserve the marital act for those who are joined by God?"

"Of course," said Jesus. "How could it be otherwise?"

Lazar looked to his lord for further clarification. None came. He looked to Brother Apollonius, who joined in the conspiracy of silence. Both masters patiently watched Lazar's face and waited for a sign that he grasped the spiritual profundity of the answer. When he finally did, the three burst into laughter.

Jesus seemed to enjoy the diversion the conversation was providing. "A physician is required to understand the workings of every organ of the body and every motivation of the mind. We certainly could not be expected to purge our patients of disease if we ourselves were ignorant of the wonders of our most primal instincts. In our community, one cannot complete medical internship without intimate and firsthand knowledge of all physical and emotional phenomena—wed or unwed, it is a necessary, indeed a pleasurable, duty. But since you have initiated such a candid discussion, what about you, Lazar? Do you remain a lamb without blemish?"

"If by that you're asking if I have known a woman, alas I have not. But my nights are restless with dreams of them, and by day it seems

I can think of little else. I most certainly intend to marry after I am raised to Perfect Master."

"Then you are fortunate that your late father entrusted you to the abbot of Carmel and not to the dour patriarch of the celibate Essenes of the Dead Sea. Otherwise, my friend, there might be no women in your future."

The friends seemed satisfied to ride on without talking for several minutes, then Lazar broke the silence.

"Master, where do you go to…when was the last time you—"

"Lazar! That will be quite enough!" This time, they both swatted him on the back of the head, and after a moment of laughter, the three rode on in silence.

"When, indeed?" Jesus thought to himself.

Jewish men were expected to marry. There were very few men as old as Jesus who remained unwed. The few exceptions were those living on the fringes of Jewish culture: hermits and members of the holy orders, the unclean, the sick and demon possessed.

As a young Carmelite physician, Jesus had the singular advantage of visiting the numerous Gentile and non-Jewish territories where gods and goddesses of fertility and pleasure were still honored. Greek and Phoenician customs permitted, even encouraged, sexual activities that might be punishable by death in Jewish quarters. Jesus found it particularly significant that in the pagan districts the instances of illnesses related to demon possession were substantially lower than in areas where Mosaic law was strictly observed.

He particularly cherished his visits to Sychar in southern Samaria where a thriving Canaanite community remained from a time before the building of the Second Temple. These worshipers of the thunder god Ba'al and his divine consort Astarte honored their passionate deities in all aspects of daily and seasonal activities. They revered the act of sexual union and celebrated it in formal and informal rites throughout the year. Any man, young or old, Canaanite or Jew, Greek or Roman, who could afford the modest price of an oblation could be treated to the delights of the Roses of Astarte, the sacred prostitutes of her cult.

About two Roman miles south of Sychar, near the plot of ground tradition held was given by Jacob to his son Joseph, stood the most sacred of the Samaritan brothels. Built adjacent to a deep and ancient well that the Samaritans called simply "the wet spot," it was known as "Jacob's well" by neighboring Jews who coveted the land and hoped someday to reclaim it. To "dip your bucket in Jacob's well" or "show charity to Jacob's Daughters" were clichés of masculine bravado acknowledged with winks and nudges by worldly men throughout Roman Palestine.

Jesus first visited Jacob's well at the age of eighteen when he accompanied Brother Apollonius on his yearly medical mission through Samaria. Throughout the first leg of their journey, Brother Apollonius tortured young Jesus with candid memories of his past visits, and Jesus pleaded for words of advice.

"You are a man now and free of vows of celibacy," the mentor assured his student. "It breaks no Mosaic law for such as you to lie with a prostitute. But remember, my young friend, the Roses of Astarte are not like the sad whores of Damascus and Jerusalem who wallow in the despair of self-hatred and spread that disease to you.

"A Jacob's Daughter loves herself as the incarnation of all that is female in heaven and earth. Their skill is such you will have no choice but to do the same. Take your time and enjoy her company. She may ask questions of you or tease you with riddles or play the harp and sing to you. If she does, be patient and enjoy, for she is disrobing your soul. It is your *soul*, not your flesh, that she will carry to paradise and take as her lover. She will make of herself an altar upon which you will gladly spill your life's blood, and in the afterglow of that sweet epiphany, you will dream dreams and see wondrous things. You will swear she sees them too as she sings soft notes that carry you from heaven to higher heaven. When you awaken, she will bathe you and oil you and give you dates and raisins to eat and engage you in Greek or Latin, about art or music, or whatever delights your mind."

Young Jesus soon discovered that Brother Apollonius was not exaggerating. His first visit to Jacob's well was indeed a journey to paradise. As reward for their healing services, Jesus and Brother Apollonius were made welcome at the Inn of Jacob's Daughters. Predictably, the Daughters lavished fervent attention on young Jesus and pretended to fight over who would first tenderly raise him to adeptship in the greater mysteries of love and pleasure.

For the next ten years, Jesus never omitted Sychar on his annual healing tour of Samaria, and he considered his friendship with Jacob's Daughters as true and sacred as those of family. He owed them more than he could ever repay. It had been three years since his last visit. He was certain that once he became King of the Jews, he would never be free to touch a Samaritan woman again.

"Lazar!"

"Yes, my lord?"

"We will change the route of our journey. Three nights hence, we will camp in Samaria at the foot of Mount Ebal."

CHAPTER TWO

Then he came to a Samaritan city called Sychar, near the field which
Jacob had given to his son Joseph. Now Jacob's well was there; and
Jesus was tired by the fatigue of the journey, and sat down by the
well. It was about the sixth hour. And there came a woman from
Samaria to draw water; and Jesus said to her, Give me water to drink.
His disciples had entered into the city to buy food for themselves.

—John 4:5–8

"I thirst. Will you give me a drink?" Jesus hoped the protocol of
Jacob's well had not changed and that these were still the proper
coded words that would initiate the sacred rite. He did not recognize the woman. She was dressed in a colorful kirtle similar to that
worn by many Samaritan women. He worried for a moment that
she might not be a Rose of Astarte.

She set her leather bucket on the lip of the well and gave him an
appealing smile. He returned her smile and sighed with relief that he
had not inadvertently offended an undedicated woman. She read his
thoughts in his sigh, and this amused her. She tossed her head to the
side and laughed politely. "What a wonderful laugh she has," Jesus
thought. It put him instantly at ease.

She raised both her hands to her temples to toss her thick black hair behind her shoulders. In doing so, she assured herself that Jesus saw the characteristic tattoos that adorned the palms of Jacob's Daughters. Jesus read *her* thoughts in this gesture and they both shared a soft laugh. The lovemaking began as a dance of wits.

Holding the skirt of her long kirtle in one hand, she gracefully moved toward Jesus until she stood directly in front of him. She was nearly as tall as he. Her breath smelled of cloves, her hair of roses. She lowered her gaze to his feet, then slowly raised her dark eyes, evaluating every aspect of his garments and stature.

"You are a Jew..." she said with a light tone of sarcastic admiration. Without losing eye contact, she reached back and retrieved her bucket and held it low against the front of her body. "...and I am a Samaritan woman." The leather was soaked dark, and it squeaked and bled as she slowly stretched its mouth wide to receive the obligatory coin. "How can you ask me for a drink?"

Jesus reached into his travel satchel and retrieved the treasury purse for the journey. It bulged with over two hundred pieces of silver.

"Is it not written that salvation is from the Jews?" he said as he dropped the ponderous bag into her bucket. So surprisingly heavy was her payment that the bucket slipped from her hands and crashed to her feet.

She did not have to look down. She knew from the sound and weight of the coins that she had just become a wealthy woman. For a moment, she broke character. She glared at Jesus, first in shocked disbelief and then with profound gratitude.

This was not what he wanted. It was spoiling the mood. He hoped they could return to their game. He cleared his voice and affected a mock accent of pious pomposity. "If you only knew the gift of God and who is the man who said to you 'Give me a drink,' you would have asked *him*, and he would have given you *living water*."

He worried for a moment that these words were too vulgar for this early stage of the contest. He soon learned his fears were unfounded. His opponent's gratitude now transformed into determination to earn her riches.

She touched his lips with the tip of her fingers. Jesus gently took her hand and moved it near his nose. It glistened with oil and smelled of mint and the sweet musk of woman. He closed his eyes and drank in her fragrance with a slow inhalation. She moved closer and placed the palm of her other hand cautiously between his legs. She rubbed him gently through his robe but soon discovered that he had not yet begun to respond to her touch.

"Sir," the woman said, "you have nothing to draw with and the well is deep. Where can you get this *living water*?" She did not remove her hand. Instead she gently probed through his garment and expertly squeezed the sleeping treasure. "Are you greater than our father Jacob, who gave us the well and drank from it himself, as did also his sons and his flocks and herds?"

Jesus closed his eyes and encircled her with his arms. He was on the verge of losing the contest of innuendoes. Without opening his eyes, he returned with a cliché. "Everyone who drinks of this water will thirst again, but whoever drinks of the water which I give shall never thirst..."

"Indeed, sir." This response amused her. She giggled and dropped her head forward, allowing her hair to brush his face and neck. She renewed her efforts with more enthusiasm, and now he grew firmly in her hand. Soon she felt empowered to lift his robe and seize him. "Oh, my lord."

Jesus knew he had to respond quickly with some witticism or be prematurely overcome with rapture. "But the water I give shall become a fountain…*springing up* to life everlasting."

The game was interrupted as they released each other in a mutual explosion of laughter that lasted several minutes. They both laughed themselves to tears and clung to the side of the well and buried their heads between their arms. They could not look at each other without escalating the hysteria. When the laughing ended, they took deep breaths and wiped their eyes and grabbed each other's hands as dear friends for whom laughter is the most intimate moment to be shared.

Grabbing her bucket of riches in one hand and Jesus's arm in the other, she led him toward the Inn of Jacob's Daughters. She rejoiced in her heart that the last service she would render beneath its ancient roof would be the gift of ecstasy to this wonderful man.

"Sir, give me this water so that I may not thirst again and need not come and draw from here." She would play the game for a few more minutes.

Jesus was ready. "Go, call your husband and come back," he teased in a tone of chastisement.

"I have no husband," she theatrically lamented with a maidenish pout.

As they entered her couch chamber, Jesus raised his finger to heaven like an outraged father. "You are right when you say you have no husband. The fact is, this day you have had five husbands, and the man who is with you *now* is not your husband."

"Sir," she said as she pushed him down at the end of her couch and kissed him firmly on the mouth. "I can see that you are a prophet." She sprang from the bed and stood directly in front of him. The game was nearly over.

"You Jews claim that the place where we must worship is in Jeru-salem…" She carefully lifted her skirt and revealed her perfumed delta of tight black curls. She rubbed herself ever so slightly and undulated her prize within inches of his face. He could not take his eyes away from it. Her fragrance was blindingly intoxicating. "*Our* fathers wor-shipped on *this* mountain…"

For once, Jesus had nothing more to say.

CHAPTER THREE

The woman said to him, I know that the Messiah (Christ) is coming; when he is come, he will teach us everything. Jesus said to her, I am he who is speaking to you.

—John 4:25–26

It was late afternoon before the autumn sun penetrated the veiled window of the couch chamber. The sheer curtain waved aimlessly in the golden light, first lifting its hem to the room's interior, then billowing out of the window like the full sail of a ship. Jesus opened his eyes and stretched his arms.

"The room breathes. We lie in a mother's womb."

"Who are you, my lord?"

"A Rose of Astarte never asks that question."

"As of today, I am no longer in service. So I will ask you again: who is it whom I have the honor of serving?"

"A man, an ordinary man—the son of a man."

"Why have you given me such a treasure?"

Jesus rolled onto his side, turning his back to her. "To ransom my soul."

There was a long pause. A soft breeze swept the curtain back into the room.

"You are Jesus the physician, are you not? You are the wonder-worker from Galilee. The others have spoken of you. They say you are a Davidian prince."

"Am I attired like a prince?" he laughed, indicating his nakedness.

"A king may choose his garment as he will!"

He rolled over and took her in his arms. "Then you must be the queen of heaven!"

"My lord, let me follow you!"

"No!"

"Why not?"

"Because it is not what I want."

"But, my lord, it is what *I* want!"

He released her and sat up. "Woman! Would you corrupt this rite with argument?"

"No, my lord. Forgive me." She sat up and reached for her garments. "Please, I did not wish to offend."

The two said nothing as Jesus robed and began to gather his things. He regretted his harsh tone and wondered why he had reacted so brusquely. He felt obliged to try to recapture the good feeling of just a few moments before.

"Well, dear friend, what will you do now?" he asked.

"I will probably return home to Bethany and live with my sister, Martha."

"Does she know that you are a Jacob's Daughter?"

"Of course. She does not approve. But our mother was also in service at the well, so she cannot protest too vehemently."

Jesus turned and carefully studied her face. Only then did he recognize the features, and he quickly turned his head to conceal his discomfort. "Your father, was he a Jew?"

She hesitated. "Why, yes, my lord."

Jesus returned to the bed and sat down facing the window. He pretended to re-lace his satchel. "A goldsmith, perhaps?"

She could not answer.

"Your father was a goldsmith, and your name is Mary."

She burst into tears and ran to kneel before him. "My lord! My lord! How do you know these things?"

"Everything in heaven and earth is connected to everything in heaven and earth." Jesus did not look down at her. He continued to stare straight ahead at the curtain. "Perhaps I am a prophet."

BOOK FIVE

THE RAISING OF LAZAR

CHAPTER ONE

These things happened that the scripture might be fulfilled, which said, Not even a bone shall be broken in him.

—*John 19:36*

It would be over soon for the two thieves. Their legs broken, the grotesque dance of death had begun. The crowd around the hill jumped to their feet and jostled each other for a better view of the suffocating felons.

"This one was near death when he was delivered up," Joseph of Ramtha commented, further distracting the centurion. "'No need to waste the nails,' they said. It appears they were right."

"Nailed at the wrists or impaled through the rectum—cru- cifixion is an art," the centurion added in a proudly respectful tone, "a veritable mystery."

At sunset, Jesus took his leave of the Inn of Jacob's Daughters and walked to Sychar to rejoin the others. In the morning, the troop con- tinued up to Jerusalem. Jesus said nothing to Lazar concerning his sis- ter. For the rest of the journey, he said very little to anyone. Nearing Jerusalem, he dismounted and silently climbed the last few miles with his disciples.

In the Holy City, the pilgrims were met by Brother Matthias, the Carmelite beloved disciple stationed there. It would be his duty to observe the crowds that followed Jesus and ferret out and identify Temple informers and Herodian agents for eventual assassination.

At first, Jesus did not receive the same public adulation he had become accustomed to in Galilee. Jerusalem was a big city and, for the most part, unconcerned with the activities of a northern holy man. Because no crowds came to him for healing, he sought out patients at the Sheep Gate, a pool of soothing mineral water where Jerusalem's lame and ill were brought to bathe. There he found a man who was too arthritic to get off his mat to enter the water. Jesus spoke a few pleasant words to him, then casually ordered him to get up and wade into the pool. Delivered from pain, the man did so easily.

"Now gather up your mat and go home, my friend. People who are truly sick need your place by the pool," Jesus joked. The man was elated at the freedom in his limbs and did as he was told. Jesus ignored the fact that it was the Sabbath, the day of enforced rest, when even the simple act of carrying one's own mat was a breach of Mosaic law. Before the man could reach his home, he was intercepted by pious neighbors who threatened to charge him for breaking the Sabbath.

The man protested that he was ordered to carry his mat by Jesus the Nazarite. The Jews rushed to the Sheep Gate to find this Jesus and have him arrested, but by the time they arrived, he had disappeared. Within the hour, the high priest Caiaphas and the enemies of the movement knew the Davidic prince was in Jerusalem.

Late in the afternoon, accompanied by his disciples and their families, Jesus went up to the Temple and spoke from the steps. The audience was openly hostile, and this frightened the Galileans. Jesus, however, seemed to relish confrontation. His knowledge of scripture and law was impressive. Again and again, he used it as a weapon to embarrass those who would attempt to trap him. As the afternoon wore on, the crowd swelled with more sympathetic worshipers who were leaving the Temple, and his words gave birth to a chorus of whispers about the holy man and his teachings.

The following day, he returned to the Temple. This time he was met by an organized band of priests and lawyers as well as a large and enthusiastic mob of people who obviously despised priests and lawyers. This day's debate was more guileful and mean-spirited. More than once, Jesus stepped dangerously near blasphemy. At one point, he likened certain lawbreakers to King David, who once ordered his starving men to break into the Temple and eat the holy shewbread.

His courage and wit soon won him the admiration of a surprising number of Romans, merchants, and curious members of various sects, several of whom offered him their homes and hospitality. This thoroughly confused the Galilean disciples, who cowered silently as their master feasted in public places and in the homes of Gentiles and Pharisees. Jesus detested the timidity of these disciples and terrorized them with acts of ever-escalating audacity. He seemed to delight in seeking out the company of whores and sodomites, tax collectors, and swine butchers.

With Brother Matthias and his men providing for Jesus's security in Jerusalem, Lazar and Brother Apollonius were free to occasionally remove themselves from the center of the action. However, they could not help observing disturbing changes in Jesus's character. On the morning of the last day of the great feast, the two shared their concerns privately at the home of Brother Matthias.

"The master seems to enjoy inflicting cruelties upon the Galileans," Lazar observed. "They are like children. I do not understand. The more he tortures them, the deeper their love—"

"And the further they plunge into delusion," Brother Apollonius added. "It is an unwholesome cycle that I fear is now impossible to break. It is he who suffers most. He hates himself for how he must use these simple people, and so he feels he must make himself worthy of that hatred. When compassion enters his heart, he tries to be truthful with them, but they misunderstand his every word. He is cursed. The more truth he reveals, the greater their misunderstanding. It was the source of his mental collapse in Capernaum. I fear the demon may never be exorcised.

"But it is not his treatment of the Galileans that troubles me now. In argument at the Temple steps, he draws increasingly from the fathomless well of mysticism. His enemies hurl pebbles of law and logic, but they fall harmlessly upon the shield of his profound understanding. Yet each time he slays with these philosophical weapons, he departs from the simple parables of the Davidic kingdom. He is losing himself in his persona and drifts into spiritual abstractions understandable to no one but himself."

The discussion was interrupted by the sound of frantic pounding upon the door to the servants' entrance. Brother Apollonius opened the door a crack. It was Brother Matthias. He burst into the kitchen and quickly turned and bolted the door. His face was covered with dusty sweat.

"Where is the master?" he almost shouted.

Lazar got up immediately and offered his seat to Brother Matthias.

"At the home of Nicodemus the Pharisee or else on his way to the Temple," Brother Apollonius answered.

"You must stop him! I bring word from Joseph of Ramtha. He warns that there is great danger in Jerusalem. Jesus must leave Jerusalem immediately."

"What kind of danger?" asked Lazar.

"Former disciples of the Baptizer, Dead Sea Essenes—they have heard that Jesus eats with Gentiles and the uncircumcised. They say he does not observe the fasts. They call him the 'wicked priest' and have convinced their elders he is a 'seeker after smooth things.' They have gone to Caiaphas and offered to support his efforts to stop the false Messiah. Zealators have been arrested. I do not know who. You must not let him go to the Temple today!"

"That may be easier said than done," Lazar said. "It is difficult to reason with the master. He seems increasingly irrational."

Matthias pounded the table with both fists. "Then all the more reason to get him out of the city! I must return immediately to Joseph of Ramtha, who is in the city on Sanhedrin business. Do I tell him that you will get the master to safety?"

"We cannot return to Galilee on such short notice," said Brother Apollonius. "The roads are watched. We will have to first secrete him nearby while we devise a plan for his safe return."

"My sisters' home in Bethany!" Lazar whispered, as if spies were in the very room. "We have yet to visit there. It is close. I am sure we can lodge there for a few days while we gather our thoughts and resources."

Brother Apollonius grabbed Lazar by both arms. "Run to the home of Nicodemus. If the master is still there, tell him of the danger. Do everything necessary to convince him to go with you to Bethany. Tell him I intend to meet him there tonight. Now more than ever he needs protection. See that Andrew and the Rock and the Sons of Thunder attend him constantly."

Lazar ran to the home of Nicodemus just as Jesus and the Galileans were leaving for the Temple. Hearing the news, Jesus was anxious to leave Jerusalem, but when Lazar suggested they seek refuge at his sisters' home in Bethany, he scowled and curtly refused.

"Master, we have no choice. By now Brother Matthias has informed Joseph of Ramtha that Bethany is where you will be. Brother Apollonius is expecting to meet us there this evening. I am sorry. We had to make plans. There was no time to consult with you."

Jesus looked into the face of Lazar and studied the strong Canaanite features he shared with his sister. Suddenly he could not help but laugh. "Everything in heaven and earth is connected to everything in heaven and earth."

"Master?"

"An Essene adage—a mystery joke. Fetch the Rock. We will go to Bethany."

Lazar located Simon and brought him to Jesus, who grabbed him by the tip of his red beard and pulled his head down so he could whisper new instructions in his massive ear. "Collect Andrew and the Sons of Thunder. Order everyone else to load their asses and return immediately to their homes in Galilee."

CHAPTER TWO

Then Mary took a cruse containing pure and expensive nard, and anointed the feet of Jesus, and wiped his feet with her hair; and the house was filled with the fragrance of the perfume.

—John 12:3

"Forgive me for disturbing you. I am Brother Apollonius. I have come from the Carmelite monastery in Galilee."

"Lazar! Something has happened to Lazar! Mary, come quickly! This man is from the monastery. Something has happened to Lazar!"

"Please. I assure you. Nothing has happened to your brother. He is fine. In fact, he is coming here this day. May I please come in and talk to you both?"

Martha cautiously opened the doors and admitted Brother Apollonius. The house was spacious, much larger than he had imagined. From the atrium, he could see a large common room and a dining room that was especially well-appointed for entertainment in the Roman style. Dominating the room was an enormous cedar table fashioned in the shape of an omega and surrounded by a dozen reclining couches. "This will be a most suitable refuge," he thought.

"I apologize if I frightened you. Lazar is quite well. He is in Jerusalem, and he asked me to come to you and announce that he will soon be here."

"Excuse me, sir, but why did he not simply come? Why does he send an angel?"

"He will not be coming alone. He wanted you to be prepared for the arrival of a very special guest, a healer and holy man, Jesus, son of Joseph the Great Carpenter."

Mary was stunned at the mention of his name. Her first thought was to run away. Her sister did not know that Jesus was their miraculous benefactor. How could she face him after Jacob's well? Would he recognize her? Did Lazar know? Would Jesus fear she might expose him? After his great kindness, she would not wish to make him uncomfortable. She wrung her hands beneath her apron and tried to listen to Brother Apollonius.

"I do not wish to alarm you, but I must tell you the master has enemies who seek his life in Jerusalem. We must soon return to Galilee, but first it is imperative that we find local shelter while we prepare security for the trip. Your brother, Lazar, is one of the master's most beloved disciples, and the dear boy suggested that you might allow us to stay with you for a few days. I realize this is a terrible imposition. I'm afraid there are seven of us in all."

"It is no imposition at all," Mary interrupted. "But is it lawful for a Jewish holy man to seek refuge in the home of Samaritan women? We are Canaanites and do not observe the fasts and customs of our Jewish neighbors."

"Our master seeks a kingdom where such distinctions will no longer separate good people. You may be assured that he will be honored to accept your hospitality."

"Then our home is the master's for as long as he needs it. He will be safe here. He may count on our discretion." Mary could not believe the words came from her own mouth.

Martha was speechless. She looked helplessly at Mary as if to say, "Do you know how much work this will be?" Mary shrugged and looked at Brother Apollonius and smiled.

"Everything in heaven and earth is connected to everything in heaven and earth," she said.

He looked at her with curious wonderment.

"A Samaritan adage," she told him.

"Then we must get to work," Martha said. "My sister is right; it will be no imposition. Since her return, we have lacked for nothing. This will allow us to share our good fortune with our brother, Lazar."

"Until they arrive, is there anything I can do to help?" Brother Apollonius gallantly offered.

"Indeed, yes," Martha promptly accepted, "in the kitchen!"

Much to Martha's disappointment, Mary excused herself, saying she needed to go to the marketplace to purchase additional delicacies. When she was gone, Martha laughed and confided to Brother Apollonius that her sister had always been a poor household helper.

Within the hour, Jesus and the others arrived at the back door. Lazar made the introductions. Jesus looked nervously about until Martha informed them that Mary was out of the house. He then politely asked if there was a chamber where he could rest apart from the others.

"Indeed, yes, my lord, and four more for your disciples. Lazar will show you. Do you remember where, dear? All of you, make yourselves comfortable. I will call you for the evening meal. Please, relax and feel perfectly free to do whatever it is you Jews do."

————

Mary spent the afternoon wandering aimlessly through the marketplace. At one point, she resolved not to return home and set out toward the home of her Jewish cousins in Jerusalem. Near the Mount of Olives, she was drawn to the shade of a street seer's awning. She dropped a coin in his hand. "Tell me my fate."

The old man placed his bony hand over his left eye and opened his right eye grotesquely wide. He licked his lips before speaking. "While the king was at his table, my perfume spread its fragrance."

"What is that supposed to mean, old man?"

"Song of Solomon, my lovely," the seer cackled lasciviously. "And what king will you anoint tonight with your tattooed hands?"

"I did not pay to be leered at and insulted."

"No, my lovely," he licked his lips again. "You asked your fate."

He then held the coin obscenely to his nose as if to drink the essence of her body that lingered upon it. Mary turned in disgust and hurried away, cursing the old lecher beneath her breath.

As she continued toward Jerusalem, she was haunted by the seer's words: "While the king was at his table, my perfume spread its fragrance." It was really quite remarkable that the old reprobate's vision would include a king at a table. Perhaps he *had* told her fate. Not twenty paces from the door of her cousins' home, she changed her mind and returned to Bethany.

She did not arrive until after Martha had served supper. She entered secretly through the servants' entrance and stood unseen behind the curtain that separated the dining room and the atrium. In her hands, she clutched an alabaster jar of spikenard. From her hiding place, she could see only three or four of the guests, all lying comfortably on their couches around the low table. Jesus, she thought, must be resting with his back to her.

In keeping with Carmelite customs, the meal was taken in silence except for quiet discussions of scripture. Mary could not see who was speaking.

"Teacher, what must I do to inherit eternal life?"

"What is written in the Law?" Jesus replied. "How do you read it?"

Mary held her breath when she heard Jesus speak. She moved slightly to get a better look and realized that he was reclining at the end of the table nearest her. Only the curtain separated the lovers. From where she stood, she could almost reach out and touch his feet. She wanted to run to him. Instead, she quietly knelt on the floor just inches away from him.

"'You must love the Lord your God with all your heart and with all your soul and with all your strength and with all your mind; and you must love your neighbor as yourself,'" the disciple answered.

"You spoke the truth," Jesus replied. "Do this and you shall live."

"But master, who is my neighbor?"

Jesus thought for a moment. Who, indeed? He looked around at Lazar and the others reclining on their couches. He thought of Mary. He wanted to see her again and worried she would not return.

"There was a man who went down from Jerusalem to Jericho, and bandits attacked him and robbed him and beat him and left him with little life remaining in him, and they went away. And it chanced a priest was going down that road; and he saw him and passed on. And likewise a Levite came and arrived at that place, and saw him and passed on. But a Samaritan, as he journeyed, came where he was, and when he saw him, he had compassion on him. And he came to him and bound up his wounds and poured on them wine and oil; and he put him on his own ass and brought him to the inn and took care of him."

Mary began to weep, for she knew he spoke of the condition of his own soul at the well of Jacob's Daughters.

"The next day he took out two silver coins and gave them to the innkeeper. 'Look after him,' he said, 'and when I return, I will reimburse you for any extra expense you may have.' Which of these three do you think was a neighbor to the man who fell into the hands of bandits?"

"Why, the Samaritan, my lord."

Hearing this, Mary's weeping became audible to all in the room. Jesus sat up and pulled back the atrium curtain to find her kneeling behind him.

"Mary!" Lazar shouted. "Forgive me, my lord, it is my sister Mary. Mary, what are you doing?"

Martha appeared from the kitchen. "Fine time to arrive, after leaving me to do all the work of this huge meal!"

Jesus laughed quietly. "Dear Martha. Do not think we are ungrateful for your hospitality. You are worried and upset about many things, but other things are more important, and Mary has chosen the good portion for herself."

Mary said nothing but fell forward to the floor and clutched Jesus's ankles and began to sob. She rubbed her face with her hands and wiped the tears upon his feet. She untied her hair and tenderly rubbed his feet and legs with the silky tresses. Seeing this intimate gesture, the disciples sat up from their couches and mumbled among themselves. Jesus stilled them with a wave of his hand.

Mary reached for the jar of spikenard and broke the ornate seal. The room filled with the fragrance of the fine perfume.

"Lord, I have—"

Jesus hushed her with the tip of his finger upon her lips. Then, as all watched in amazed silence, she poured the entire priceless contents of the jar upon his feet. It was an act of insane extravagance. Lazar looked to Martha.

"Is she mad? Where did she get the money to buy such a thing?"

Before she could answer, Simon the Rock spied the tattoos on Mary's hands. "Whore! Whore! Master, she is a whore. Surely you can see what she is. You allow her to touch you like this?"

"She is my sister, you splutter of pig shit!" Lazar jumped up on the table and leapt upon Simon's back.

Simon spun and heaved his titan bulk so violently that Lazar was thrown to the wall. Andrew lunged at Mary and tried to pull her away from Jesus, but was stopped by Brother Apollonius, who snared his neck with the tablecloth then fell upon him, smashing his nose against the floor. Lazar returned to his feet and lunged again toward Simon.

"Stop! Stop it! All of you!" Jesus stood up and helped Mary to her feet. He escorted her to the kitchen where Martha stood crying in the pantry. He returned to the dining room and silently surveyed the mess. "Simon, see to your brother's injury. James, John, clean this place and repair what damage you can. Quickly! The four of you will leave this night for Galilee. I will join you when I can again stomach the sight of you."

A few hours before dawn, Simon the Rock, Andrew, and the Sons of Thunder left Bethany. By noon, they had rejoined their families and the remainder of the disciples walking north on the road near Jericho. They were too ashamed to reveal why the master had banished them.

When Rhoda asked Andrew how he broke his nose, he only growled and answered, "*Samaritans.*"

CHAPTER THREE

Now Jesus loved Martha and Mary and Lazar.
—*John 11:5*

The days that followed the unpleasantness and the Galilean disciples' departure were surprisingly agreeable. As always, Brother Apollonius was the soul of discretion, and Lazar and Martha wisely resolved never to pursue the circumstances of Mary's relationship with Jesus.

Each day, Lazar walked to Jerusalem to gather news from Brother Matthias. While he was gone, Brother Apollonius and Martha conspired like matchmakers to give Mary and Jesus time alone together in the house. They went to the marketplace or busied themselves in other parts of the house. This was not a burden for Brother Apollonius, who found himself increasingly attracted to Martha. It wasn't long before Mary and Jesus were conspiring to give Martha and Brother Apollonius time alone together.

Jesus loved this taste of domestic life, and even more, he loved awakening each morning without a past or a future. For a brief moment, he fantasized about the joys of a householder. The bliss became nearly unbearable the evening of Lazar's eighteenth birthday. Martha prepared his favorite dishes, and both women talked of their mother and shared precious memories of baby Lazar. Jesus and

Brother Apollonius had tales to tell also. After all, they had known the lad since he was six years old.

"If I were on the mountain now, I would be eligible to be raised to Perfect Master," Lazar boasted to his sisters.

"You are still eligible," Brother Apollonius chuckled. "You are just not on the mountain."

"But masters, what if I am never to return? These are terrible times, and the future is uncertain. Perhaps my days will end prematurely. Is there nowhere but the mountain where the ceremony can be administered?"

"These matters are tiresome to your sisters. See how they yawn," Jesus said, obviously trying to change the subject. "Perhaps we will discuss it later."

The following day when Lazar had left for Jerusalem and the women were at the market, the two Perfect Masters discussed the feasibility of raising their friend to the sublime degree. Jesus doubted the ceremony could be successfully executed under field conditions, but Brother Apollonius was anxious to at least explore the possibility.

"In ten years on the mountain, you and I officiated at the raising of nearly forty Perfect Masters. Not one perished. Even the abbot said he had never seen a more talented initiatory team."

"But we are not on the mountain. Remember what is involved. Even under ideal circumstances the ordeal is nearly as strenuous for the officers as for the candidate."

Jesus was not exaggerating. The ceremony whereby "man is raised from death to life" was a complex and grueling marathon. Even for the skilled adepts of the Carmelite monastery, the procedure was fraught with danger.

For twenty-eight days prior to initiation, the candidate was isolated from the community in a windowless chamber and tutored by the meditation master. Each day he was allowed to drink only a small amount of rainwater and eat only a spoonful of paste made of mashed apples, raisins, and royal honey.

The daily routine was relentless in its tedium: two hours of instruction, two hours of meditation, one hour for food and bathing, two hours for sleep. After three days, even the most attentive candidate could no longer reckon the hour or the day. Within a fortnight, he found it hard to discriminate between waking consciousness and dream. After three weeks, the words of the meditation master took visible form in the mind of the candidate and echoed as visual images across a screen of perpetual twilight.

Three days before the ceremony itself, the instruction period was discontinued, and the candidate was allowed to recline on the floor while the master led him on a guided meditation of death. At this point, his consciousness could be plucked from his body like an overripe fig and guided through the wondrous and terrible membranes of postmortem existence.

With the meditation master acting as psychopomp, he was led in vision to the very threshold of absorption into the godhead. Extreme care was taken, however, to terminate the sessions before the supreme instant of ecstatic dissolution. It would be necessary for the pilgrim to take *that* step alone during the final ordeal.

The candidate had no idea when the day of his initiation had arrived. The routine was followed as usual, but on that day, his food was laced with a powerful drug made from the gall of a venomous fish. Within seconds of swallowing his last supper, he suffered profound paralysis—his breathing stopped, his body temperature dropped dramatically, and his heartbeat became imperceptible. To all outward appearances, he was dead. At this point, only the most experienced observer could determine whether or not physical death had actually occurred. The master physician was called into the chamber to examine the body and to solemnly declare, "Our brother is dead."

Meanwhile, the helpless candidate remained entirely conscious of everything that was said and done around him.

The "body" was then laid out, bathed, and wrapped with spices in strips of linen in accordance with Jewish burial customs. Each act was accompanied by song or recitation of scripture: "'Precious in the sight of the Lord is the death of his saints.'" Followed by a procession of convincing mourners, the "body" was then paraded outside the monastery gates and taken to the necropolis, there to be laid upon a shallow shelf carved in the wall of a tomb "'...for death is the destiny of every man.'"

For three days, the "body" lay motionless in the cool silence of the grave. To keep from going mad, the candidate was compelled to fling his consciousness outside the shell of his paralyzed corpse. His only salvation was to reenact the death meditation over and over again until he crossed the final threshold to consummate the supreme marriage of human consciousness with that of the divine.

If all was done correctly, on the afternoon of the third day the venom was neutralized by the natural defenses of the candidate's body. Then, in a meticulously choreographed ceremony, the master physician reanimated the candidate's lungs with a skillfully delivered blow to the chest. When normal breathing resumed, the meditation master removed the burial wrappings and grasped the newly raised Perfect Master firmly by his right hand and wrist. As he pulled him up to embrace him, he whispered the vivifying word in his ear. This supreme word could never be uttered in life except by a person serving as master in the act of raising a candidate.

Although Jesus wanted to arrange this supreme experience for Lazar under the proper circumstances, he remained sadly resolute. "Much as we love our friend, I am afraid it would be impossible for you and I alone to raise him."

"Hear me out," said Brother Apollonius, "then I will say no more."

Jesus nodded.

"I am certain that within a short walk from this house we could secure a small house or building suitable to safely isolate Lazar for a month. I am also certain that you and I together, working in shifts, could serve as both meditation master and physician."

"Perhaps," Jesus agreed. "But it might kill us both."

"We have the ceremony memorized. We have done it many times before. We do it better than anyone. I know where I can secure fresh venom, and I already have at least half of the embalming materials in my bag. The rest I can purchase locally."

Jesus tried to be patient with this line of argument. "I concede that all you say is true. Perhaps we could find a house and prepare Lazar for the great crisis. What do we tell his sisters while all this is happening? We certainly cannot compromise the secrecy of the rite. If we overcame that problem, where on earth do you suggest we bury him? There is no Essene necropolis in Bethany."

"We will tell his sisters that he has fallen ill with a contagious disease and he must be isolated for at least a month of treatment. Our efforts, of course, will fail, and then we must sadly inform them that the lad is dead. As for the burial, I admit it would not be easy. Failing all else, we could purchase a suitable tomb in the community necropolis south of Bethany and inter him there. Everything would take place exactly as it would at the monastery except that the processional mourners would actually believe Lazar is dead."

Jesus was outraged. "What a monstrous hoax to suffer upon Martha and Mary! They would never forgive us!"

"Never forgive the man who raised their brother from the dead?"

Jesus threw his hand in the air as if to wave away a fly. "This discussion is ended, my friend."

At that moment, Lazar entered through the servants' entrance and shouted to see who was home. Jesus made their presence known in the dining room and asked why he had returned so early. Lazar appeared at the kitchen entrance. His garment was torn and covered in blood, and he was bleeding severely from a cut over his right eye. Seeing this, the two older men rushed to his aid. As they proceeded to dress his wound, he shared his story.

"Matthias and I were nearly captured by Temple soldiers near the Mount of Olives. There have been more arrests. Five Zealators were stoned to death this morning outside the palace of Caiaphas. For his own security, Joseph of Ramtha has severed communications for at least a fortnight. His last message to you urges you to stay where you are if you are safe. Our enemies believe you have returned to Galilee.

"Also, there has been an ominous turn of events. I fear we may be undone. As unbelievable as this may sound, many of the aged Essene fathers and former enemies of our Plan now see the momentum of the times and are supporting a coup. But they say they will never recognize *you* as king. They tell their followers you are a bastard because you were born between the two betrothal rites. Many are now calling you the 'evil priest.' They say your brother James is the lawfully born Messiah."

"Now, when we should be fighting the Romans and the Herodians, we turn like children and fight ourselves," Jesus said sadly.

Brother Apollonius was furious. "But it is Jesus, not James, who has fattened the flock for the last two years. It is Jesus who heals the sick and casts out demons and feeds the hungry!"

"'Supernatural tricks of the "evil priest" to deceive the elect,' they say. They laugh and say that the flock has a short memory, that you will lead them to 'smooth things.' The Dead Sea elders charge that of late Jesus has done nothing but outrage the Pharisees and sup with the unclean."

Brother Apollonius looked Jesus straight in the eyes. "Perhaps they would see him raise the dead?"

"I beg your pardon?" Lazar looked puzzled.

From the side garden, Jesus heard the voices of Martha and Mary as they greeted neighbors on their return from the market. In seconds they would be in the house. He looked helplessly at Brother Apollonius. He saw his life and the hopes of his friends and elders unraveling before his eyes. He was losing the kingdom, and now he was bringing danger, perhaps death, to his loved ones.

Martha and Mary were at the threshold. Jesus could hear the sound of the bolt sliding back.

He squatted down in front of Lazar's chair and gripped his hand with the token of his degree. He spoke softly but with great haste. "Illuminated Brother Lazar, you have been tried by this assembly of Perfect Masters and found worthy to undergo the supreme ordeal. Knowing that the consequence of this ceremony is death, is it your unequivocal will to proceed?"

For a moment, Lazar could not grasp what was happening. Then it struck him. He looked up at Brother Apollonius, then back at Jesus. "Oh, yes, my lords. Yes!"

"Then your will be done. Consider the ceremony begun. You will follow our instructions without question. When your sisters arrive, they must believe that you are gravely ill."

Brother Apollonius rushed to the door and stopped Mary and Martha in the kitchen and pushed them back through the door.

"Ladies, you cannot enter. Your brother has fallen seriously ill. See here his blood on the doorstep. It issues from his bowels. It is a highly contagious malady. It can be deadly, but the master and I have had experience with it. We must immediately remove Lazar from your home and isolate him from the community until his contagion passes."

The women were stunned and demanded to see Lazar. From within the house, he shouted to his sisters, "Martha, Mary, please, do not come in. Listen to the masters, please!"

Jesus joined Brother Apollonius at the doorway. "Mary, I am afraid we must impose upon you further. Without alerting the neighborhood, we need you to secure for us an isolated house near here. We can pay whatever is necessary, but you must do it quickly. Your brother's life depends upon it."

"If he must be isolated, then let it be here. Martha and I can stay with our cousins in Jerusalem for as long as necessary."

This alternative had not occurred to Jesus or Brother Apollonius. It was ideal. They immediately accepted Mary's offer.

"I am afraid you must leave right now. Brother Apollonius will escort you to Jerusalem to learn your location. He will visit you there in a few days and bring you what you might need from here. Whatever you do, do not come back here or send anyone else. And do not tell anyone that Jesus has been here. When this is over, we will send for you and help you cleanse your home. I am sorry, but this must be."

Jesus turned and entered the house. He shut the door behind him and stood perfectly still and listened as Brother Apollonius tried to comfort the sisters. Lying to Mary was the most difficult thing Jesus had ever done. When he was sure the sisters had gone, he walked through the house and carefully examined each chamber.

The largest room in the house was the lavatory. Obviously constructed to Roman tastes, it housed an enormous communal bath. A large double door opened to the courtyard and well. The chamber was also accessible from two parts of the house: one door opened from the kitchen, one from a short hall adjacent to the master sleep chamber.

Jesus decided that the master sleep chamber would serve as Lazar's cell for the month-long ordeal. Its proximity to the lavatory made it ideal, for Lazar would be required to ceremonially bathe each day.

He moved a few unnecessary items from the chamber and then called Lazar.

"Illuminated Brother, this room is your temple. You will leave it only when instructed. Do you understand?"

"Yes, my lord."

"Illuminated Brother, you shall now bathe yourself in cold water and dress in coarse linen. The windows of this temple shall be sealed against the light. It will remain bathed in darkness—for the temple shall no longer illuminate you, but by *you* must it be illuminated."

CHAPTER FOUR

Now there was a man who was sick, Lazar of the town of Bethany,
the brother of Mary and Martha. This is the Mary who anointed the
feet of Jesus with perfume and wiped them with her hair. The Lazar
who was sick was her brother. His two sisters therefore sent to Jesus,
saying, Our Lord, behold, the one whom you love is sick. Jesus said,
This is not a sickness of death, but for the sake of the glory of God,
that the Son of God may be glorified on his account.

—John 11:1–4

Lazar was the perfect candidate. He fell immediately into the
bizarre routine of fasting, meditation, bathing, and sleep. Jesus and
Brother Apollonius, however, got off to a rather clumsy start. On
the mountain, they were assisted by two aides who supervised the
meal and bath periods. Without this extra assistance, they found
themselves drifting helplessly into the rhythm of Lazar's cycle. By
the third day, they were both nearly exhausted and realized they
would have to reorganize the schedule of their shifts to better
accommodate their own daily sleep patterns.

The second week proceeded flawlessly. Jesus became totally
absorbed in the ceremony and pushed the cares of the revolution
from his mind. Twice during the week Brother Apollonius had time

to walk to Jerusalem to visit Martha and Mary and buy necessary items at the market.

Late in the evening of the sixteenth day, Brother Apollonius took it upon himself to seek out Brother Matthias in Jerusalem. To his great surprise, he found him at home meeting with Joseph of Ramtha and Ephron of Arbela. The four conspirators embraced like excited schoolboys. Then, realizing that Brother Apollonius was alone, Joseph of Ramtha broke the circle and demanded to know where Jesus was.

"He is safe. He ordered the Galileans home, and we are staying with Lazar at the home of Lazar's sisters in Bethany. For over a fortnight the good women have been lodging with relatives in Jerusalem while Jesus and I..." Suddenly, Brother Apollonius realized how absurd his words were going to sound to Ephron of Arbela, who was not an initiate. "...while Jesus and I raise Lazar to Perfect Master."

Ephron stared blankly at Matthias and Joseph of Ramtha, thinking at first that he was being teased.

"What?" Matthias asked sharply, not believing his ears.

"It is true. The procedure is more than half complete. I take full responsibility for convincing Jesus to officiate. The boy is most deserving. We all owe him so much, and his...we all know he may never return to the mountain—"

"Enough," Joseph of Ramtha said calmly. "Obviously, Lazar has been tried by a lawful assembly and found worthy to undergo the supreme ordeal. It is useless for us to now debate the wisdom of the timing. The ceremony must continue, but I am afraid it cannot proceed with Jesus as meditation master."

Brother Apollonius started to protest, but Joseph did not allow him to speak. "Sit down, brother. These have been eventful weeks. There are things you must know. Caiaphas has suspended arrests until he determines exactly who is really supporting him. The Dead Sea elders have for the moment ceased their vilification of Jesus until they decide who they hate more: Caiaphas, Herod, or the Romans. Herod has become mad with guilt and is now openly lamenting the execution of John. He is even hinting that he might support Jesus. He has issued an invitation for Jesus to come to Sepphoris to entertain him with a miracle at court."

"This is wonderful news," said Brother Apollonius. "Is this not the chaos we dreamed would precede the ascension?"

Joseph laughed cynically. "Yes, but this is all happening *one year* ahead of schedule. Our alliances are not firm. Less than half of our confederates are in place at Temple and at court. There are still many dangerous weeds that must be plucked by the Zealators."

"But I do not understand why, for the next fortnight, Jesus cannot quietly continue as Lazar's meditation master. We plan to raise the boy at the community necropolis. It must be Jesus who performs the act. It will be seen as his greatest miracle!"

Joseph of Ramtha suddenly raised his hand to silence the two monks. He stood up and turned to Ephron of Arbela with a smile.

"My friend, we beg your understanding. Would you be so kind as to allow us old fanatics a moment to privately discuss the claptrap of our foolish ceremonies? I am sure such a discussion would only weary you."

"Of course," Ephron said. "Discuss your tokens and secret words in peace. I could use a breath of midnight air."

When Ephron was gone, Joseph's countenance changed to that of pure rage. "You would defile the supreme rite with a public display? Are you both insane?"

"My lord, it will be exactly as upon the mountain." Brother Apollonius knew he could not match either the wit or the wisdom of Joseph of Ramtha. Still, he was resolute in his conviction. "No part of the ceremony will be compromised or revealed to the profane. Yes, the mourners will think the boy is dead, but in three days, they will see Jesus, the heir to the throne of David, walk into the tomb and bring him back to life. When Jesus and Lazar emerge from the tomb, there will be no more talk of 'evil priest' or 'smooth things,' and the followers of James will certainly not witness *James* raising the dead."

Joseph lifted his hands to his temples and ran his fingers through his silver hair as if to prevent his brain from exploding.

Matthias only smiled and whispered, "Yes, Joseph. Yes. There may be no other way."

Joseph said nothing but nodded his head as if agreeing with some inner voice. When he finally broke the silence, he spoke softly and with great deliberation. "Are you positive that a suitable tomb can be secured at the community necropolis?"

"Yes, my lord, yes—if I have to purchase an entire acre. Yes."

"And if the boy actually dies? It would destroy the Messiah. All would be lost."

"The lad is strong. In our years on the mountain, Jesus and I resurrected nearly two score without fatality."

Joseph rolled his head from side to side to relieve the tension in his neck, his mind weighing the many possibilities. Finally, he announced, "Then the Jews shall see the master raise the dead in Bethany. But I am afraid someone else must be his meditation master until resurrection day. Jesus must return immediately to Cana to muzzle his insipid Galilean disciples. Ephron of Arbela has been visited by an angel from the north who tells him that Andrew, the Rock, and the Sons of Thunder have gone to Cana and are staying at the estate. He will tell you."

Joseph opened the door and looked out into the darkness for Ephron. He spied him across the street near the stables, urinating in the moonlight.

"When you are empty, my friend, come into the house and fill our brother with news of the Galilean simpletons."

Ephron's news was not good. Instead of returning to their own homes in the north, the disgruntled disciples took it upon themselves to go to Cana. There they hoped to enlist Mary's aid in returning her mad son to Galilee, and thence to his senses.

"The beloved disciples and resident pupils are understandably confused and upset, and the continuing presence of the blathering Galileans is bringing unwanted attention to the compound. Simon the Rock is even presuming to teach the pupils in Jesus's name. It would be amusing if not so dangerously absurd."

"This must be stopped," said Joseph, "and only Jesus can do it. He must go to Cana immediately to restore order. There is time for him to do what needs to be done and return in time to raise Lazar, but he must go to Cana *now*! My two guards will accompany him."

"But who will help me with Lazar?" Brother Apollonius interjected. "I cannot conduct the marathon ceremony alone, especially in the critical last days."

"I will help you," Matthias said. "I was an aide for two raisings. I cannot serve as meditation master, but I can supervise the food and bathing periods and visit the market and be your angel should you need one."

Joseph slammed his hand upon the tabletop. "It is settled then. Matthias, take my horse and carry word to my guards to come here immediately. When you return, we shall all go to Bethany and tell Jesus. Until then, I advise Brother Apollonius to take a nap. For the next twelve days, he will have precious little time for sleep."

Brother Apollonius did not get much rest. Within two hours, he, along with Matthias, Joseph of Ramtha, and his guards, were back in Bethany. So as not to disturb Lazar's meditation, they met with Jesus in the stable.

Jesus laughed and shook his head when told of the Galileans' behavior. Reluctantly, he admitted that he would have to go to Cana to bring them under control. Before departing, he and Brother Apollonius calculated the precise day and hour when Lazar must be raised. Brother Apollonius suggested the Galileans return with Jesus to Bethany to witness the resurrection. He vowed to dispatch an angel to Cana to bring word that Lazar was near death and a second angel who would meet Jesus and the others on the road a day later to announce his "death."

———

When Jesus reached Cana, he discovered the reports of misbehavior among the Galileans had been somewhat exaggerated. It was true that Andrew, the Rock, the Sons of Thunder, and a handful of others had taken up residency at the compound, but their presence evoked only amused concern among the beloved disciples, and very few of the pupils took anything they said seriously. Mary was overjoyed to see her son and joked that she would continue to feed his playmates forever if it meant he would stay home.

The Galileans were also happy to see their master and showed canine-like willingness to submit to his chastisement for their behavior in Bethany. But Jesus's mood had shifted. He was no longer inclined to torture them. Instead, he used his days in Cana to reestablish their love and trust. He even allowed them to be instructed by the beloved disciples and join the resident pupils in daily meditation and exercise.

When the first angel arrived from Bethany with word of the seriousness of Lazar's condition, the entire compound was concerned, but no one more than the Rock, who feared he might have injured the lad during the fight in Bethany. He pleaded with Jesus to depart for Bethany immediately to heal him. Jesus knew that if they left immediately they would arrive before Lazar was entombed. To the utter dismay of the disciples, Jesus waited two days before agreeing to return. With an entourage of twelve, they finally set out up the Jordan Valley for Bethany.

Early on the third day of their journey, the second angel intercepted them with the news that Lazar was dead. The twelve disciples were devastated. Jesus appeared unmoved and declared Lazar was only sleeping. They took little comfort in the words and looked to each other as if the master was slipping back into madness.

At the pace the retinue was traveling, Jesus reckoned he would arrive at Bethany around midmorning on the third day of the burial. The resurrection must occur late in the afternoon, but Jesus would first need time to meet with Brother Apollonius and learn the location of the tomb. Also, he knew he would have to face and comfort Mary and Martha. He dreaded the thought.

CHAPTER FIVE

Now Bethany was towards Jerusalem, a distance of about two miles.
And many Jews kept coming to Martha and Mary to comfort their
hearts concerning their brother.

—John 11:18–19

Are you the feet?
   No, I am not.
When you have no feet?
   I am that which remains.

Are you the legs?
   No, I am not.
When you have no legs?
   I am that which remains.

Are you the phallus?
   No, I am not.
When you have no phallus?
   I am that which remains.

Are you the hands?
   No, I am not.
When you have no hands?
   I am that which remains.

Are you the arms?
    No, I am not.
When you have no arms?
    I am that which remains.

Are you the flesh?
    No, I am not.
When you have no flesh?
    I am that which remains.

Are you the bowels?
    No, I am not.
When you have no bowels?
    I am that which remains.

Are you the lungs?
    No, I am not.
When you have no lungs?
    I am that which remains.

Are you the heart?
    No, I am not.
When you have no heart?
    I am that which remains.

Are you the spine?
    No, I am not.
When you have no spine?
    I am that which remains.

Are you the brain?
    No, I am not.
When you have no brain?
    I am that which remains.

Are you the blood, the bones, the sinews, the hair?
    No, I am not.
When you cast no shadow?
    I am that which remains.

Lazar lay motionless on the floor of his chamber. He was unaware the day of his initiation had arrived. For nearly a week he lingered in perpetual trance, following the voice of Brother Apollonius as it led him step-by-step through the progressive portals of the death meditation. At each threshold of consciousness, he was barred by a terrible vision, an aspect of deity in the form of an archetypal beast. During the final days of the meditation, Lazar memorized the name of each guardian and a divine word by which the specter could be dispelled. It was an old technique, far older than the Carmelite sect. The abbot once confided to Brother Apollonius that he believed the words of power were of Egyptian origin and that the death meditation had been used in the black land for millennia to assure the eternal life of kings.

Brother Apollonius was pleased with Lazar's progress. He had thoroughly mastered all the names and words, and for the last three days had journeyed flawlessly to the highest levels permissible before the great climax.

Brother Matthias entered the darkened chamber and helped Lazar to sit up. Brother Apollonius elevated the silver bowl before Lazar's eyes and offered the customary prayer of thanksgiving. "Supreme and terrible One, bless this food unto our bodies, bestowing upon us pure and everlasting sustenance."

He dipped a small silver spoon into the poisoned paste and held it before Lazar's lips. "In your mouth be the essence of the light and of the darkness."

"In my mouth be the essence of the light and of the darkness." Lazar opened his mouth and received the sacrament.

Brother Apollonius next elevated a tiny chalice. The wine would activate the venom and the great ordeal would begin. "In your mouth be the essence of the great sea, the womb wherein all men are begotten and wherein they shall rest."

"In my mouth be the essence of the great sea, the womb wherein all men are begotten and wherein they shall rest." Lazar took the cup to his lips and swallowed. Instantly his chest was seized with a paralysis that spread like an icy fire to his extremities. He heard the cup fall to the floor but was unable to move his eyes to see. He slumped forward into the arms of Brother Apollonius, who gently lowered the helpless body to the floor. Brother Matthias closed Lazar's gaping eyes, but it did not matter to Lazar. Eyes open or closed, his consciousness translated every sound, every word into a vivid internal visual display.

Once Lazar was stabilized, the two Perfect Masters chanted the Spell of Passing. Brother Apollonius started, and Matthias answered:

He has no feet.
> He is that which remains.
He has no legs.
> He is that which remains.
He has no phallus.
> He is that which remains.
He has no flesh.
> He is that which remains.
He has no bowels.
> He is that which remains.
He has no lungs.
> He is that which remains.

He has no heart.
> He is that which remains.

He has no spine.
> He is that which remains.

He has no brain.
> He is that which remains.

He has no blood, no bones, no hair.
> He is that which remains.

Our brother casts no shadow.
> He is that which remains.
> He is that which remains.
> He is that which remains.

The two Perfect Masters immediately set to work. There was much to be done. They first moved the body to the lavatory and gently bathed it. They then anointed it with oils and spices and wrapped it with broad strips of linen. Throughout the entire procedure, Brother Apollonius chanted the traditional funeral prayers. This was a new chore for him. On the mountain, the chants were performed by an unseen chorus of novitiates.

When Lazar's body was wrapped and respectfully laid out in the bedroom, they proceeded to return Mary and Martha's house to normal. They scrubbed the lavatory, removed the window coverings and all vestiges of their makeshift initiatory temple. It then became Brother Apollonius's sad duty to walk to Jerusalem and inform Martha and Mary that Lazar was dead.

Before leaving Bethany, he went to the home of the hazzan and purchased (at a somewhat exorbitant fee) a suitable excavated rock tomb in the community necropolis.

Things did not go as smoothly in Jerusalem. Martha and Mary were inconsolable. Mary pounded her fists on Brother Apollonius's

chest and demanded to know how Jesus the great healer could aban-
don her brother as he lay dying. It was more than Brother Apollonius
could bear.

He told her an angel had been dispatched in her name to fetch
Jesus and encouraged her to be strong. But his words were of no comfort. Martha and Mary's cousins, however, were very excited to learn
that the famous holy man of Galilee might soon appear in Bethany.
They wasted no time in sharing the news with their Jewish neighbors.
By the time the sisters set out to return to their home in Bethany,
they were followed by a crowd of nearly forty.

Lazar made a convincing corpse. He was wrapped in linen strips
that had been soaked in nard and other spices in a manner not unlike
the burial rites of the Egyptians. He was laid on the bare wooden
platform of the bed in the master sleep chamber. Curtains were
drawn over the windows, and the chamber was lit only by three floor
lamps, two at the foot of the bed and one at the head.

When Martha saw her brother's body so displayed, she whim-
pered like a little girl. Mary stood motionless at the foot of the bed
and remained coldly silent as if attuning to her brother's repose. Matthias and Brother Apollonius made no attempt to assuage their grief.
Except for a few details, the procedure was now out of their hands.
There would be no more coaching, no more guided meditations, no
more chanting. The actual sounds of grieving would now be the only
outside impressions to bombard Lazar's consciousness. Martha and
Mary did not observe the Law, but in the eyes of their Jewish relatives
and neighbors, the house would remain unclean until the body was
removed and the rooms ritualistically cleansed.

Shortly after sunrise, Brother Apollonius fetched the hazzan to
supervise the final tasks and oversee the interment. By noon, Lazar
lay on a shallow shelf hewn in the wall of the small cave at the north-
ernmost edge of the necropolis. Brother Apollonius managed to

spread two woolen blankets upon the rough ledge before the body was placed. Lazar's back and neck would appreciate this thoughtful act in the days that followed his resurrection.

The entrance to the cave was unusually small and could have been sealed with a relatively small stone. The hazzan bewailed the fact that, due to the short notice, he was unable to have a small stone roughly hewn. He suggested to Brother Apollonius that if he wanted the tomb sealed immediately, he could purchase a larger, more expensive stone that was immediately available. Brother Apollonius scowled and paid the hazzan his extra money and had the great stone rolled into place. Lazar would remain entombed for three days. Until Jesus appeared, there was nothing to do but wait.

Early the next morning, the sisters' house was surrounded with strangers posing as grieving well-wishers. Martha and Mary recognized only a small fraction of those who had gathered, most of whom made little attempt to conceal the true nature of their interest in Lazar's home.

"What is he like—the holy man from Galilee? Was Lazar his disciple for long?"

"I regret that I did not know your brother. Was he with the magician when the water was turned to wine?"

"We have heard he is a great healer. It is such a pity. Perhaps he could have healed the dear boy—have you thought of that? It is so sad."

"I would very much like to meet this Jesus. I have heard he will be visiting you. Do you think he will come today?"

————

Brothers Matthias and Apollonius maintained a very low profile. The sisters did not introduce them to the other visitors, nor did they reveal their relationship with Lazar. The following day saw even more gawkers from Jerusalem. The neighborhood took on the surrealistic atmosphere of a festival, with scores of people loitering in the street in front of the sisters' house. By eavesdropping on their conversations, Brother Apollonius learned that many of them fully expected Jesus to appear and attempt to raise his friend from the dead.

"This must be Joseph of Ramtha's doing," he thought.

Matthias pointed out a handful of agents of Caiaphas. They made no pretense of mourning, nor did they try to enter the house, but simply positioned themselves near the front threshold.

Just before sunset, two young men raced past the house as running angels. "Jesus, the Davidian prince, is camped with his disciples by the Jordan near Bethabara. He will pass through Bethany in the morning."

Word spread immediately. One of the agents of Caiaphas hurried back to Jerusalem to inform his master. Those who were preparing to go home at dusk instead settled down where they stood or sought nearby shelter. No one, it seemed, wanted to miss the arrival of the holy man from Galilee.

In the early evening, Apollonius and Matthias strolled past the necropolis and satisfied themselves that all was secure. They watched the silver bow of the moon follow the sun behind the Mount of Olives. They then returned to Martha and Mary's garden and rested outside near the lavatory wall. They said little to each other as they listened to the prattle of the assembled throng. Finally, they agreed to take turns sleeping and bade each other good night.

Throughout the night, a steady trickle of new arrivals turned the neighborhood into a campground of sleepy pilgrims. Some built small fires in the middle of the street. Others clung to each other between buildings or under trees. By daylight, there wasn't a yard or doorway unoccupied.

Brother Apollonius awakened Matthias shortly before dawn. They quietly stripped and proceeded to bathe themselves from a bucket of cold well water. They could hear Martha and Mary arguing in the house. Suddenly the lavatory door swung open and the two found themselves standing naked and shivering before Mary's wrathful glare.

She shook her head at them. "Perfect Masters...eh? When you two are through baptizing each other, you can come in the house and get something to eat. We are told he comes today. We will want to do the proper thing."

CHAPTER SIX

And Jesus was in tears.
—*John 11:35*

"Do you think he will come to the house with this multitude surrounding us?"

"I do not know, Mary," Brother Apollonius answered. He took silent comfort in the knowledge that after today he would no longer have to lie to Martha and Mary. "The crowd outside is filled with the agents of our enemies. We have been told that those who sought his life in Jerusalem have for the moment ceased their persecution of him, but we must all remain vigilant. He might still be in danger."

"He will most certainly wish to pray at Lazar's tomb," Matthias said. "I am sure he will come here first to show his respects."

Mary folded her arms and nervously bit her lip. "I will remain here until the sun is overhead. If he has not arrived by then, I will seek him on the road from Bethabara. If his life is in danger, I wish to be near him."

Brother Apollonius said nothing. He had resigned himself to let the events of the day unfold as they would. His immediate concern was Lazar's health. The paralyzing effects of the venom would be dissipating. If the boy had succumbed to panic and not sought refuge in the death meditation, the last four days would have been an unspeakable claustrophobic nightmare. Even now he might be struggling to free himself from the burial cerements, his heart seized with fear, his mind wracked with hallucinations. It was a horrible thought. Even more unthinkable was the possibility that the poison had actually taken Lazar's life. He remembered the words of Joseph of Ramtha: "It would destroy the Messiah. All would be lost."

Shortly after breakfast, the crowd hummed with reports that Jesus and a dozen of his disciples had broken camp by the Jordan and were heading toward Bethany. A handful of children ran down the road in hopes of being the first to see them coming, but returned within the hour with nothing to report.

———

On the road, Jesus looked up and squinted at the midmorning sun. By high noon they would be in Bethany. The path rose steeply as they neared the town. Simon and Andrew trudged silently at his side. The Sons of Thunder and the rest trailed listlessly behind.

"Master, will we be seeing Lazar's sisters?" asked Simon.

Jesus answered with a cold glare that made Simon avert his eyes. "We will visit their home first."

"Master, I am too ashamed to speak with the sisters. Will you please tell them of my sorrow that Lazar is dead?"

Jesus stopped in his tracks and turned to face the train of disciples. When they were all in view, he shouted, "Simon grieves that Lazar is dead. I tell you all again…Lazar is sleeping! Do you hear me? Lazar only *sleeps*, and I shall awaken him. Do you not believe this? Do you not believe in me?"

"I do, Lord. I believe in you," Simon answered. The Sons of Thunder echoed, but the others only mumbled half-heartedly. Jesus smiled. For a moment, he actually enjoyed the idea of raising the dead.

———

"The sun is at its zenith. Martha, go to the necropolis and wait. I will go to meet Jesus." With those words, Mary veiled her head, marched out her front door, and pushed her way through the watchful crowd. For a moment, the mob did not know which sister to follow. About half of them elbowed each other for the honor of being first in line behind Mary. The others, including Matthias and Brother Apollonius, fell in about fifty yards behind Martha, who was headed to the necropolis. Matthias surveyed the crowd and estimated the number at over one hundred.

"The more witnesses the better. This should please Joseph of Ramtha," Matthias whispered.

"Yes, but we must not let this mob hinder his arrival at the tomb. If they chose to stop him, there is nothing we could do," Brother Apollonius answered.

———

Lazar's right leg spasmed violently and tore against the dampened linen. His bladder and bowels emptied, and the foul contents soaked through the fabric. Slowly, as if emerging from a pool of warm water, he became conscious of his environment. He struggled to open his eyes. He could not. His body was still paralyzed. He struggled to remember the initiation, the death meditation, the sacraments, the sound of the wine cup hitting the floor.

I am that which remains. I am that which remains. Our brother casts no shadow. I am that which remains.

He tried to take a deep breath to reinhabit his body, but as yet he had no control of his breathing—he realized he was not breathing! He began to panic.

I am that which remains; I am that which remains.

Suddenly, memory of the death meditation returned. He had passed the pylons. He had defeated the guardians.

I am not afraid. I am not the breath; I am that which remains.

An echo of the supreme moment rang through his soul like the pealing of a great bell.

I am not the bell. I am that which remains, the ring of the pealing bell.

His chest spasmed, and his abdominal muscles cramped in knots. He took notice as if it were happening to someone else...some*thing* else.

Perhaps it is dying. Let it, if it will. I am that which remains.

————

"Run, master! They have come to kill us." Andrew seized Jesus by the arms and pulled him behind Simon and the Sons of Thunder. "Run! We will cover your escape."

"They will not harm me. Behold! Those that greet us are led by Mary, the sister of Lazar."

Jesus pushed his way to the forefront of his entourage. Mary picked up her pace when she saw Jesus. After only a few steps, she threw back her veil and started to run. Jesus did not run to her, although he wanted to. He continued with measured, theatrical steps until he stood face-to-face with Mary. He desperately wanted to tell her that Lazar was alive and all would be well. He was at a complete loss for words.

She fell at his feet and cried, "Lord, if you had been here, my brother would not have died."

In the eyes of the Galilean disciples and those who followed behind Mary, the scene was poignantly tragic. Jesus was struck dumb with emotion. He looked up at the sun to reckon the time.

"Where have you laid him?" he shouted for all to hear.

"Come and see, Lord," the crowd replied in one chaotic voice.

Jesus helped Mary to her feet. Suddenly, the two found themselves enveloped by the mob. For a moment, Jesus worried he would not be allowed to move.

"Take me to the place where he sleeps," he shouted over the tumult.

The crowd heaved forward as a single organism that rumbled like the drone of a monstrous insect. The excitement was so tangible that Jesus felt as though he was being carried aloft by the great vibration. He could not feel the earth beneath his feet.

Then, in an instant, everything stopped. Jesus stood again upon the dusty earth. Directly before him the crowd split to the left and right, revealing the pitted landscape of the necropolis. Standing before the sealed tomb, like a chiseled monument of a goddess of mourning, stood the veiled figure of Martha.

Jesus wept.

The people murmured, "See how he loved him!"

But some of them grumbled, "Could not he who opened the eyes of the blind have prevented this man from dying?"

"Take away the stone!" Jesus shouted.

"But Lord," said Martha, "by this time his body stinks. He has been dead four days."

"Take away the *stone*!" Jesus shouted louder so that all could hear.

The Sons of Thunder pushed their way through the crowd and put their shoulders to the stone and rolled it away. Jesus stripped off his outer garment and climbed through the narrow entrance of the cave. He stood for a moment to let his eyes adjust to the light. Martha spoke the truth; the body did indeed stink. Jesus sniffed the air and smiled with joy. Human piss and feces never smelled so sweet. The foul perfume meant that Lazar was alive.

Jesus quickly moved to Lazar's side and began to unravel the linen strips that wrapped the head and face. He then loosened the swathing around the neck, chest, and wrists. Lazar was still not breathing, but the presence of sweat under his nose told Jesus that the venom had become impotent. He linked his fingers to make a double fist, then pounded twice in rapid succession upon Lazar's chest. He then pushed firmly on the boy's abdomen. A dark brown plug of mucus shot out of Lazar's mouth, and the young man gasped for air. Jesus laughed with joy and relief. Lazar coughed and again gasped for air. He could hear Jesus laughing. Through his coughing, he started to laugh also.

Control was coming back to Lazar's body. He rocked madly from side to side. Jesus quickly freed his arms and unraveled the coverings of the right hand. He gently pushed Lazar back down on his back and pressed his ear to the boy's chest to assure his heartbeat and breathing had returned to normal. He then grasped Lazar by the right hand and wrist and pulled him to a sitting position. Putting his lips to Lazar's right ear, he whispered the secret word of the Perfect Master—the sacred token that is uttered only from the lips of one Perfect Master to the ear of another on the occasion of being raised from the sleep of the dead.

"Thank you, lord," Lazar said between coughs.

Jesus smiled. "Perfect Master, thank you."

"What day is this?" asked Lazar.

Jesus smiled as he hurriedly unwound the remaining wrappings around Lazar's legs. "Resurrection day, dear brother. And the world awaits your dawning light. I am afraid we have not kept this moment very private. In fact, my friend, today it is *you* who shall be the most famous man in Roman Palestine."

"I do not understand," Lazar said as he moistened his dry mouth.

"You will understand in a moment. Wait here until I call you out."

———

Jesus appeared at the mouth of the tomb. The crowd fell silent; then, seeing he was alone, began to mumble among themselves. A few started to disrespectfully chuckle. Jesus took a few steps toward the crowd and glowered at the scoffers. They fell silent.

Mary pushed her way to Jesus's side and clutched his arm and started to speak. "Master, come. Come home now."

Jesus gently released her grasp. "Hush now, my dear. Your brother was only sleeping. He has now awakened. You will see. I will call him out."

Jesus turned to the tomb. "Lazar! Lazar! Arise! Come forth! *Come!*"

There was no movement from within. For a moment, Jesus feared that Lazar had fallen back into unconsciousness. After all, the young man had been without solid food and water for many days.

Simon, Andrew, the Sons of Thunder, and the Galilean disciples fell to their knees while Brothers Matthias and Apollonius pushed their way to Jesus's side.

"Lazar! Arise!—and come forth!"

Finally, after what seemed an eternity, a thin shadow crossed the mouth of the tomb; then Lazar appeared. A bit wobbly, his eyes pinched tight against the brightness of the late afternoon sun, he did not immediately see the astonished host of witnesses to his resurrection.

"Lazar! Come!" Jesus repeated his command so the lad might better locate him among the throng. Eventually, Lazar spied Jesus standing with Mary. A tiny smile cracked his face—a face that had been paralyzed for over three days. He stumbled awkwardly toward Jesus. With each unsteady step, the murmur of the crowd grew louder until finally it burst into a thundering roar as he fell into the waiting arms of Jesus and Mary. The three remained in tight embrace while nearly all the stunned witnesses fell to their knees and broke into songs of praise to God and the prophets.

"A miracle of God!"

"Jesus has raised the dead!"

"A miracle!"

"A miracle! He is a prophet!"

"He raises the dead!"

"Messiah! We are delivered!"

"Elijah!"

"Our Davidian Prince! Hail! Hail our deliverer!"

"Our savior! Our king! Our king!"

"All hail King Jesus! Jesus! King of the Jews!"

Upon hearing these words, the joy in Jesus's heart turned instantly to terror. He knew that among the onlookers were spies and agents of Rome and Caiaphas. He turned to Brother Apollonius, whose eyes told him he was thinking the same thing.

"This miracle will be the death of me."

BOOK SIX
CRUCIFY HIM

CHAPTER ONE

Many of the Jews who had come to Mary, when they saw what Jesus had done, believed in him. And some of them went to the Pharisees and told them everything Jesus had done.

—John 11:45–46

The rabble was too overcome with religious rapture to take much notice of Matthias and Brother Apollonius as they quickly spirited Lazar, Jesus, and the sisters away from the necropolis and into the narrow backstreets of Bethany. Simon and the Galilean disciples realized that they, too, must follow.

For the time being, Mary and Martha's home would be the only place for all of them to immediately seek refuge. It was close to the necropolis, and the people knew it was Lazar's boyhood residence. Still, it was a dangerously awkward arrangement. It would only be safe for a few hours, and other plans must immediately be made. They all arrived within minutes of the resurrection.

Mary and Martha wasted no time smothering their still-some-what-confused brother with sisterly kisses and tears. He assured his sisters that Jesus had indeed awakened him from the sleep of death, but before Lazar could continue with his postmortem narrative, Brother Matthias brought everyone back to cold reality.

"The sun is nearly set. It will be only a matter of minutes before the house will be surrounded by the mob from the necropolis."

Jesus ordered the Galileans to stay in the common room. They were still in awe of Jesus, and they sheepishly obeyed without discussion. Jesus took the sisters by the arms, and together with Brother Apollonius and Matthias, ushered a still-dazed Lazar into the lavatory area and began to strip him for bathing. Matthias asked the sisters to bring water, wine, and salt. Jesus and Brother Apollonius gently pushed Lazar down on his back on the flat draining stones of the floor and began to vigorously rub his limbs with wet sponges. Brother Apollonius took the wine from Mary, lifted the boy's head, and bade him to drink a few swallows. Once they were sure the wine stayed down, Jesus clutched a handful of salt and plunged it into the pitcher of water and swirled it into a solution, which he then poured down the lad's throat until he gagged, then violently vomited. The sisters were alarmed, but Matthias assured them, "Fear not. This is good. He is purging himself of the venom of the underworld."

When Lazar was steady enough to stand, Jesus, Brother Apollonius, and Matthias had one final duty to perform as officers of Lazar's initiation. Jesus asked the sisters to please leave the lavatory for a moment. They reluctantly obeyed.

Brother Apollonius reached to where he had stored his own toiletries and produced a neatly folded white linen robe of a Carmelite Perfect Master. Jesus helped Lazar to his feet, and the three slipped the robe over Lazar's naked body and softly, alternatingly, whispered, "We three... "

"Receive thee...

"As Perfect Master!"

Matthias then kissed Lazar on the left cheek and whispered, "The Kiss of Life."

Then Brother Apollonius kissed him on the right cheek and whispered, "The Kiss of Death."

Finally, Jesus kissed him on the lips and gently exhaled his own breath into Lazar's lungs; Jesus then waited for a moment to allow Lazar to return the breath of life back. Jesus then broke the kiss and whispered, "Hail unto thee, twice-born Perfect Master, he who dreads not life, for he knows there is no dread afterlife."

The four Perfect Masters paused only for a moment of silent joy. The commotion that was building outside in the street brought their attention back to earth. "Bring him out! Bring him out!" The chant was incessant but eerily respectful.

"Caiaphas's spies are among the throng," Matthias whispered. "Lazar must at least make a brief appearance before the rabble, but what shall he say to escape the snare of blasphemy?"

Jesus smiled almost sarcastically and put his arm around Lazar's back. "Brother Perfect Master, you have one small chore to discharge before you sleep tonight. Perhaps the words of the book of Job might serve both to soothe the sheep and defang the wolves?" Lazar was a keen student of the Tanakh; he knew exactly what Jesus was suggesting.

Before they rejoined the disciples in the common room, Apollonius took Jesus by the arm and whispered, "Let us allow Lazar to appear alone with the twelve disciples. Let the Galileans be the ones to share the glory. To them, the miracle is real. We must ignite and exploit their faith, for they are the face *of* common people and the face *to* the common people. Also, it will divert attention from us." Jesus acknowledged the wisdom of this advice and nodded his agreement.

The disciples fell to their knees when Lazar and the others reentered the common room. The Rock groveled most pitifully and reached to touch Lazar's feet. "Forgive me, dear brother. Forgive me. Please. I struck you. I insulted your sister. Forgive me."

Lazar calmly took him by the hands and raised him. "Come, my brother. Come with me…all of you. Let us bear witness to our neighbors." Lazar unlatched the door and allowed the Galileans to exit before him. Jesus, Matthias, Brother Apollonius, and the sisters remained inside the house.

The narrow lane in front of the sisters' house was packed shoulder-to-shoulder with curious neighbors and spies. When Lazar appeared in the doorway, the crowd became eerily still. Many fell to their knees as if even the slightest ripple of disrespect would break the spell that held Lazar to the land of the living.

Lazar stepped forward and stretched his arms to his side and turned full circle as if to confirm his living stature. He then stepped toward the witnesses nearest him, who recoiled slightly as if they might catch fire at his touch. "Come! Touch me. Am I not living flesh?" One or two reached forward and lightly touched his hands and arms and excitedly affirmed the warm, corporeal status of the lad. Lazar then held up his hand in a silent blessing and simply said, "'For there is hope of a tree, if it be cut down, that it will sprout again, and that the tender branch thereof will not cease.'"

Listening from inside the house, Jesus, Matthias, and Brother Apollonius broke into wide smiles of admiration for Lazar's brilliant scriptural allusion. It was the perfect thing to quote, for there was nothing specific that Caiaphas's spies could seize upon as being a blasphemous admission of supernatural healing or seditious threat to the Temple establishment or the Romans.

At the same time, the disciples and the general population would immediately interpret the words as an unspoken but unambiguous confession: "Yes. I was dead and passed into Sheol. But the Lord Jesus, the miracle-working holy man, raised me from the dead."

And perhaps most importantly, to the ears of the restless and militant, and for the benefit of all who even now stood ready to lay down their lives to end Roman and Herodian rule, Lazar's words were a clear signal that the revolt was at hand—that there was hope that the corrupted "tree" of the puppet kingdom of Herod would soon be cut down, but that it *would* sprout again as the tender branch of the true bloodline of King David in the person of his direct descendent, Jesus Ben Joseph.

"Bless you all," Lazar said. "Please return to your homes. Bless you."

The crowd reverently obeyed, and Lazar turned and reentered the house. The disciples silently followed. The spies hurried directly to the house of High Priest Caiaphas to give full account of the extraordinary events of the day.

Also among the crowd was a most unusual spy. Inconspicuously cloaked as a Jewish matron, she was accompanied by a maid servant and two muscular male companions whose modest tunics discreetly concealed Roman short swords.

CHAPTER TWO

So the high priests and the Pharisees gathered together and said, What shall we do? For this man does many miracles. If we allow him to continue like this, all men will believe in him, and the Romans will come and take over both our country and our people.

—John 11:47–48

"Sleep now. We will depart before dawn for Ephraim." Jesus almost barked the orders to the twelve disciples. Still bathing blissfully in the reflected glory of Lazar's near-celestial performance, they silently obeyed and found space on the floor and against the walls of the common room.

Neither Brother Apollonius nor Matthias had been in contact with Joseph of Ramtha in over a week. They could only guess what he and the Council of Seven had heard about Lazar's resurrection or how this new development might affect the timing of the Plan. One thing was certain: Jesus and the disciples could not stay at the sisters' house. Sunrise must find them gone from Bethany and away from Temple spies and potential assassins.

The village of Ephraim was only about ten miles northeast of Jerusalem and was home to a trusted agent of Uncle Clopas. If Jesus and the disciples could get there undetected, they would likely be safely concealed until the Council of Seven could meet.

As the disciples and the sisters slept, Jesus, Apollonius, and Matthias busied themselves with packing. It was decided that Lazar would not accompany them to Ephraim. Instead he would remain for a few days in Bethany with his sisters to circulate among the neighbors as "living" testament to the miracle.

It was deep midnight when Jesus crept into the bedchamber where Mary and Martha were sleeping. He stood quietly and gazed at Mary and realized how much he loved her—how much he enjoyed her company, how joyfully she triggered his manhood, how being with her these last few months had enriched his soul, how he never wanted to be without her. He knelt by her bed and kissed her forehead. She awoke and smiled.

"You are going," she whispered sleepily. It was not a question.

"I must. But I will return—or else I will send for you shortly." He paused for a moment. "Mary. We *must* be together."

This sudden declaration left them both paralyzed for a moment. Neither said a word for an uncomfortably long while. Jesus finally broke the silence. "Mary, when I come into my kingdom...or perhaps even before I come into my kingdom, I wish us to be wed...if you agree, that is."

She laughed quietly and raised her head and kissed him. "Yes, my lord. I think I shall agree." She kissed him again, then gently guided his hand to the warmth of her belly. She placed her hand over his and whispered, "I carry your child. A child for the new kingdom?"

For a moment, Jesus could think of nothing but the implications of this joyous and terrifying news. He smiled and kissed Mary once more. "Of course! Indeed! Indeed!" It was all he could think of to say. They both shared a nervous laugh. They both knew very well that Martha overheard the entire conversation.

"Now! You must go!" Mary ordered in a mock tone of wifely authority.

Jesus joined Brother Apollonius in the common room.

"You look pale, my friend. Are you unwell?"

"Yes. Yes. I mean…No. I am fine," Jesus answered. "We will discuss it later."

They joined Matthias, who was quietly awakening the sleeping twelve. Within moments, they had all gathered their things and slipped silently into the night—northward toward the hill country of Ephraim.

———

Martha rolled over and smiled at Mary. (She had heard every word.) "They have gone?"

"Yes. But he will return."

CHAPTER THREE

When the governor was sitting on his judgment seat, his wife sent to
him and said to him, Have nothing to do with that righteous man;
for today I have suffered a great deal in my dream because of him.
—*Matthew 27:19*

Jesus and the others arrived at the Ephraim house without incident
and found it to be more spacious and comfortable than they had
expected. Much to their surprise, they were met there by Jesus's own
brothers, James and Judas. Since Jesus's last stay at the Cana head-
quarters, the two brothers had developed a sincere interest in the
spiritual teachings carried on by the Carmelite agents. James especially got along well with the Galilean disciples. Like them, he was
plainspoken and provincial in his manner and attitudes. He had a
talent for interpreting Jesus's spiritual messages into simple terms. It
was clear that as Jesus was becoming increasingly subtle and inscrutable, James was actually enjoying his role as shepherd to the common folk.

The Council of Seven had not yet taken James into their full con-
fidence but had already begun discussing his possible role after the
coup.

Jesus had just finished his morning meditation in the garden
when an angel arrived from Jerusalem with a message from Uncle

Clopas asking that Jesus and Brothers Apollonius and Matthias meet him and Joseph of Ramtha at his country home in Ramah the next day at high noon. The angel added that they must keep this message and their destination secret from everyone, especially the Galilean disciples. Jesus sent the angel back affirming they would be there.

The town of Ramah lay southwest of Ephraim, just a few miles directly north of Jerusalem. Uncle Clopas owned a modest cottage and stable there. It served as a quiet retreat where he occasionally lodged whenever business brought him to the Holy City.

The three arrived shortly before high noon to find the house empty except for Lazar, who met them at the door. Jesus was very pleased to see the young man. "Lazar! You are looking remarkably well for a man who had been dead for three days. What is this about?"

"I assure you, I do not know, lord. An angel came to Bethany yesterday and summoned me. He told me nothing except that I was to come and I was to tell no one."

"How are your sisters? Mary, is she well?" Jesus blushed a little when he heard the words escape his lips.

Lazar smiled. "Yes, lord. She is well indeed."

The three had just finished washing their feet when Joseph of Ramtha and Uncle Clopas arrived on horseback. The two were dressed very modestly, more like tradesmen than nobles. Something was obviously wrong. Uncle Clopas was not his gregarious self, and Joseph looked positively ill, lines of care etched deeply into his ashen face. He appeared twenty years older than he had only a few weeks earlier.

Clopas spoke first. "Friends. Friends. Please. Let us sit. We have much to discuss, and I'm sorry to say it is very disturbing news. Very disturbing."

Joseph sat at the head of the table and patted his hand nervously on the tabletop. He cleared his throat. "I don't know where to begin."

"Ephron," Clopas reminded him. "Start with news of Ephron."

"Yes, of course. Ephron. Three nights ago, our beloved council member, Ephron of Arbela, was beset on the road by Temple soldiers and brought before Caiaphas. Caiaphas's personal guard then bound him and put him to the question regarding the intentions of the miracle worker of Galilee. The interrogation was brutal and lasted throughout the night. I regret to report that before he died, Ephron laid bare the essential secrets of the Council of Seven and our great plan."

The words were so blunt and absolute, no one in the room could speak. It was though all the air had been sucked from their bodies.

"Just like that? We are discovered? It is over?" Lazar snapped.

"I'm afraid so, dear boy," Clopas replied.

"We are undone," Jesus uttered beneath his breath.

"Yes. We are indeed undone," Joseph repeated.

"How do you know all this has occurred? Are you certain of these facts?" Apollonius asked.

"Quite certain, indeed," Joseph responded. "For the last two years, my own agent...*our* own agent...has served as personal valet to Caiaphas. There is nothing the high priest does or says that is not almost immediately made known to me. And I say to you, Caiaphas now knows *everything*...enough to successfully thwart the entire Messiah movement and have us all put to death the moment he so chooses, and I have every reason to believe he will soon choose to do just that! The only thing that is preventing our immediate arrest is the fact that Caiaphas must avoid dispatching us without inadvertently implicating himself and the Temple establishment in the eyes of the Romans.

"Friends, as of this moment, we six are the only ones privy to this information. I'm afraid it is an inescapable fact. The sacred cause for which we and our forefathers plotted and fought and died is now doomed, at least for our generation. We in this room must accept that fact and immediately proceed to make new plans, first to save our lives, then to set the stage for the next generation's opportunity. All our thoughts and labors must now be bent toward a *new purpose*..."

"And what exactly *is* this 'new purpose' for which we must now dedicate our lives?" Jesus asked with more than a hint of sarcasm in his voice.

Clopas answered, "The preservation of your blood, my boy—and the universal recognition among Jews throughout the world that, crowned or not, you truly are the King of the Jews, that *you* carry the throne of David in your loins and that it is only a matter of time until the kingdom will come again. My boy, no matter what happens to us, *you* must live, and your seed must sow the fields of the future."

Jesus's thoughts turned instantly to Mary and the child.

Joseph leaned forward and placed his hand on Jesus's. "A thousand male infants were butchered by Herod the Great when you were born, and countless more martyrs shall surely fall in the coming holocaust, but *you*, my boy...you must live."

"But lord, what *is* the coming holocaust you speak of? Is this the revolt of the Zealators? How can you be so certain the future holds such a catastrophe?" Lazar asked.

"Yes! How, indeed?" Apollonius could no longer hold his indignation. "My lord, it is easy for you to say we must now bend our labors toward a new purpose, but do you *really* believe any of us will be able to escape with our lives? The demons that seek our destruction are legion: Herod, the Romans, the Sadducees, the Pharisees, the Dead Sea Essenes, the priests, the money changers, and a host of greedy landholders who now covet your family estates and fortunes! They all hate us, and all want us dead! Our only chance of survival was the *success of our plan*! Now that it has been taken from us, what hope remains?"

"Ah, yes!" Joseph responded. "The demons *all* hate us. But their hate and fear might be our salvation, for they hate *each other*...and they *all* fear the greatest of devils: Rome!"

Jesus stood up and tried to appear calm. "May the doomed king speak? May the blood of David speak?"

The comment actually made Uncle Clopas and Lazar almost smile.

"I would like to hear the answers to Lazar's question and Apollonius's concerns. But first, tell us, Joseph, how is it you are privy to *Rome's* intentions? Is Pontius Pilate's valet your agent?"

"Better than that!" Clopas shouted. "Please, Joseph. We must tell them now. Please tell them of our abduction."

Joseph rubbed his eyes with his fingertips as he always did when trying to gather his thoughts. He cleared his throat and began. "Two nights ago, Clopas and I were dining at my home in Jerusalem when an angel brought word of the capture and death of Ephron of Arbela. As I was escorting the angel to the door—"

Clopas interrupted Joseph in mid-sentence. "As he was seeing the angel out, the door flew open, right in Joseph's face, and knocked him to the floor. Four or five...I think it was five...it might have been six...fully armed Roman soldiers poured into the room, their swords drawn, saying, 'Clopas Ben Heli! Joseph of Ramtha! You will come with us!'

"They led us to a covered cart and blindfolded us. Two soldiers remained with us in the cart, and we were carried some distance. I thought for certain we were about to meet the same fate as poor Ephron. When we finally stopped, the soldiers helped us out...quite gently actually...and guided us a few paces and then removed our blindfolds. We found ourselves in the most delightful torchlit garden. Refreshments and delicacies were spread pleasantly on a long marble table, and we were asked to sit on the most comfortable—"

"Never mind the refreshments!" It was Joseph's turn to take over the story. "We were met in the garden by a statuesque vision of feminine beauty gazing at us with the saddest, most enchanting eyes. She spoke, almost as if she were in a dream. She apologized for our inconvenience. Then, without further pleasantries, she introduced herself:

'I am Claudia Procula, daughter of Julia, the daughter of Caesar Augustus. I am the wife of Lucius Pontius Pilate, governor of this nightmare corner of the empire. Perhaps you've heard of him?' She did not wait for an answer.

'Unlike most Roman husbands and wives of our class, we are profoundly devoted to each other. He has never denied or disrespected my wishes. We are of one mind and hide nothing from one another, for I have *a gift*. I have sent for you this night because I wish to save your lives and the life of the wonder-working holy man you are grooming to be *King of the Jews*.'

"The lady sat down on a garden bench and began to lightly twirl a ringlet of her hair.

'Like many in my family, I suffer the falling sickness. It is a curse, but it is also a key to my great *gift*. Indeed, since coming to Judaea I rather look forward to my episodes of divine madness, just so I can for a few timeless moments escape my crushing ennui. For the past year, whenever I am plunged roughly into the spirit world, I am rescued by a sweet specter who is my physician. He comforts me, soothes me, encourages me, but most of all, he shows me visions of events that are yet to be and counsels me as to what I must do here in the world of flesh and bone.

'When first I heard rumors of the miraculous deeds of Jesus, I sensed him to be an emissary of my spectral counselor. When word reached me he would come to Bethany to raise the dead, I visited the necropolis to see for myself. The moment he appeared to my sight, I recognized him to be the very same counselor of my visions.

Our fleshly eyes met for only a moment, and in that instant, the veil between the two worlds fell away and I understood he and I to be one in spirit. I realized he needed *me* as much as I needed *him*. I am his angel of protection.

'That is why I must talk to you gentlemen. My husband and I know everything you think we could not possibly know. We know that all your bickering little cults are terrified of this supernatural Jesus. How foolish they are, don't you think? My husband and I know that at this very moment these silly sects are jostling each other to have him arrested and killed, and we know that if nothing is done to stop them, these boorish fools will succeed.'

"She stood and walked to the refreshment table and daintily poured two goblets of wine and handed them to us.

'I presume you know that last evening your high priest, Caiaphas, tortured to death one of your Council of Seven and that he revealed your entire plot to overthrow King Herod Antipas and reestablish a Davidian theocratic monarchy. Is this not so? A pure-blood David on the throne? Yes? I must say, gentlemen, I am impressed by the level of sophistication your planning displays.

'Please, gentlemen, my time tonight is short, and I still have much to share with you. Your Messiah movement is compromised beyond reclamation, at least for the next few years. If you cannot see that, then I have vastly overestimated your intelligence. Your fellow conspirators have been unmasked and are at this moment in mortal danger. You must now accept your circumstances and aim the dart of your will toward securing your own survival.

'My dear fellows, I think it is important for you to understand that my husband harbors no ill will toward Jesus or you or even the idea of your little dream kingdom. But allow me to be frank with you. The *timing* of your little revolution is making him very nervous. His imperial appointment as governor of Judaea will soon come to an end. The gods so far have allowed him to administer a modest semblance of Pax Romana in this hellish corner of the empire. He cannot and *will not* have his golden reputation besmirched in the final months of an otherwise successful posting. No, gentlemen! He and I will return to Rome with our heads held high and our purses full. I have seen it. I have a *gift*.

'The spirits have shown me what will come to pass, gentlemen. I am destined to save the life of my sweet physician Jesus, and in doing so, I will incidentally be helping you salvage your precious dream of a future Jewish kingdom. But! It is a kingdom that must wait until my husband has successfully completed his posting in Judaea. Your kingdom must wait until he and I are once again safely ensconced in our villa in Pompeii.'"

Brother Apollonius spoke up, "My lords, this is indeed a tale! My head is swimming. Tell us, Joseph, what must we all do now and in the days to come? Did this Roman seeress tell you exactly *how* she and her husband were going to save us all?"

Joseph rubbed his eyes again. "Yes, but for the moment only broad generalities. The mechanism has many moving parts and the drama peopled with many players with many motives. The scheme is hopelessly complex and will likely be beset with many surprises. There are always factors infinite and unknown, and we must be prepared to be audaciously courageous and flexible to every twist of plot. But the lady assures us that she has spent her entire adult life exploiting chaos to create order. As long as we keep in intimate contact with her, Pilate will be ready to adjust to every unexpected event."

Joseph filled everyone's wine cup and sat back down at the table. He lowered his voice.

"Caiaphas knows we are planning for Jesus to fulfill the prophecies and enter the Holy City in triumph a few days before the feast of

Passover. Word has already gone out that this is going to happen, and already a host of devotees are planning an enthusiastic welcome.

"Our valet-agent informs us that Caiaphas plans to allow this to happen so as to further incriminate our Messiah in blasphemy and sedition. He will then wait for Passover, when we are all gathered together in the Holy City. Then he will strike and have Jesus arrested and quickly tried and publicly executed."

"So, Lord Joseph, tell us: how do we prevent that from happening?" Jesus asked with a smile.

"We don't prevent it," Joseph answered coldly. "We will allow that all to happen. You will be arrested, tried, and executed."

Jesus's smile faded.

"And then, my son, you will raise yourself from the dead."

CHAPTER FOUR

And all the acquaintances of Jesus stood afar off, and the women who had come with him from Galilee, and they were beholding these things.

—*Luke 23:49*

And about the ninth hour, Jesus cried out with a loud voice and said, Eli, Eli, lemana shabakthani! My God, my God, for this I was spared!

—*Matthew 27:46*

All was quiet except for the sounds of the labored breathing of the three condemned. Even the crowd at the base of the hill was mute. Mary, the sister of Lazar arrived, accompanied by Jesus's mother, her sister Ruth, and the wife of Uncle Clopas. It broke the women's hearts to see Jesus so cruelly displayed. Mary tried to comfort herself with the knowledge that, if all went as planned, in four days she and her son, along with the sisters Mary and Martha, would be safely aboard one of Uncle Clopas's ships, bound for Smyrna, then on to Gaul and the safety of the Diasporic community.

Mary was almost grateful. She had become tired of the whole sad affair. She offered a silent prayer of thanks for Pontius Pilate. His willingness to arrange a mock execution of the "King of the Jews" in exchange for the secret deportation of this troublemaker did not come cheaply. Her Cana estate was now the property of Rome, and dear old Uncle Clopas's businesses were now in the hands of new and demanding Roman partners. He, too, would be joining the family in exile.

"Why did they have to beat him so? Look at him. He's lost so much blood," Mary said under her breath.

"The people must be convinced the execution is carried out," whispered Ruth. "But see, your son is only tied to the beam. His flesh will soon heal. You'll see, my lady."

Mary's eyes brightened for only a moment, then she sank to her knees and wept. Seeing this, the crowd around her began to mumble and stir.

Jesus opened his eyes and looked down upon his mother and loved ones. He wished they would go away. It was bad enough he would not fulfill the dreams of his father and the efforts of generations, but to be mocked and scourged and spat upon, to be made to hang naked, to suffer for the rest of his days the shame and oblivion of foreign exile…He groaned through his pain…

"My God. My God. For this I was spared!"

CHAPTER FIVE

So the soldiers came and broke the legs of the first, and of the other
who was crucified with him. But when they came to Jesus, they saw
that he was dead already, so they did not break his legs.

—John 19:32–33

The thieves yielded up their souls within moments of one another.
The centurion and his sergeant watched patiently as the two car-
casses surrendered the contents of their bowels, then hung limp.
The two Temple soldiers were visibly shaken by the sight and stood
transfixed before the gruesome finale.

Joseph of Ramtha, Lazar, and Brother Apollonius moved quickly
toward the cross of Jesus and covered his arms with the burial cloth
so that witnesses below could not see that his hands would not be
ripped from nails. Lazar, from atop a ladder, found it impossible to
untie the ropes on the left side of the beam. He called to Apollonius
for a blade to cut them. Before he could respond, the centurion drew
his own short sword and delivered it up to Lazar, who nervously
hacked through the rope before handing the weapon back to its
owner. Apollonius hastened to position himself between the soldiers
and the cross to discourage their scrutiny of the body. Once the feet
were freed, Lazar slowly lowered his master's body down to the arms
of Apollonius, who laid it gently on the ground.

The centurion ordered his sergeant to remove the other two victims. The swarthy veteran seemed to enjoy his work, and he executed his task with grim efficiency, first by detaching the heavy horizontal beams, then letting them fall violently to the ground, the hands and arms still nailed to the planks. The torsos flopped forward with such force, the nailed feet ripped free from the base of the vertical beam. When he was finished, the sergeant sat down, took a swig of water, then started to boast to the Temple soldiers of his distinguished life of carnage.

"I swear it is true. I have been nine years with the legion. I have seen thousands of dead men. They quickly swell." He took another swig of water. "They will *sing* to you if you coax them in the gut with your spear. Sometimes, if they don't like you, they splutter a fart for you through the wound."

The older of the two Temple soldiers shook his head in disgust. "Hush, Roman! The dead are unclean. We Jews do not skewer them for amusement."

"To your feet! Anatomy class is over." The centurion had little respect for the grim topic of conversation. "On your feet, sergeant! Help these men entomb the middle carcass."

The sergeant jumped to attention. But before going to help Lazar, Joseph, and Apollonius with the limp body of Jesus, he picked up his spear and turned to the Temple soldiers.

"Watch this," he said with a broad, toothless grin. "I'll show you what I mean."[12]

---

12. Editor's note: The main narrative of the Egyptian scrolls abruptly ends here and is followed by the "Epilogue of Clopas" (which also appears at the end of both the Mount Carmel and Toulousean manuscripts). For sake of continuity (and to avoid reprinting the epilogue three times) the epilogue will appear only once at the very end of this book.

CHAPTER SIX[13]

But one of the soldiers pierced his side with a spear, and immediately blood and water came out.

—John 19:34

"No!" shouted Lazar.

"Stop! Stop!" screamed Brother Apollonius and Joseph of Ramtha.

But it was too late. The Roman thrust his spearhead deep into the side of Jesus's torso, creating a liplike wound just below the right nipple. Jesus did not move. The sergeant laughed obscenely, then stared blankly for a moment and cocked his head as if to listen to the body. He seemed genuinely disappointed that the corpse did not emit an entertaining death flatulence. Brother Apollonius pushed the brute aside and quickly threw the burial shroud over Jesus's body.

Joseph knew he had to act quickly. He shouted at the centurion, "The sun is setting. Do what you must with the other two. Pilate's order instructs us to remove this one before the Great Sabbath begins at dusk. His tomb is yonder. This is my property. We three will inter him before your man further desecrates our dead!"

---

13. Editor's note: Both the Mount Carmel scrolls and the Toulousean duplicate narratives continue here.

"My apologies, Lord Joseph." The centurion appeared genuinely contrite. "I'm aware of Pilate's orders. Please. Care for your dead as you see fit."

Brother Apollonius and Lazar rolled Jesus's lifeless body onto a plank and carried it the few short yards to the newly hewed cave. Joseph followed, making a loud and dramatic show of lamentation for the benefit of the witnesses, who now were beginning to disperse.

Once inside the tomb, Apollonius lit a small oil lamp and quickly examined the body. He uncovered the wound and wiped the blood from the opening to get a better look.

"The bleeding has stopped, but there is water draining. The blade may have missed the heart, but we won't know if the lung has been pierced until his breathing resumes." He paused and stuck two fingers in his mouth, wetted them with his saliva, then slipped them deep into the wound.

"The drug is strong. If the heart is beating, it is imperceptibly weak. Joseph, I do not know! He might still be alive. We won't know for several hours when breathing continues. What shall we do? If he lives, this injury will restrict his movement for days, perhaps weeks. It will be difficult to move him. He certainly won't immediately be able to travel by sea. He will need time to recover somewhere nearby. If he is alive, that is."

Joseph pinched his lower lip and mumbled to himself while organizing his thoughts before giving voice to them. "Rome needs a dead king. The cults need to be confused and paralyzed by a divine mystery! The kingdom needs to continue dreaming of a living bloodline of a savior king."

He gently laid his hand upon the crown of Jesus's bloody head, then leaned down to whisper in his ear as if he were listening. "Dead or alive, that is what we shall give them…is it not so?…Jesus Ben

Joseph, Ben Heli...? Dead or alive you shall...you *must* live eternally in the imagination."

Joseph stood straight and looked at Lazar and Apollonius. "So! We must now proceed as we arranged with Pilate. The tomb must be found to be miraculously empty when the family reopens it for purification."

Joseph stared silently at the body for what seemed an excruciatingly long moment, then he turned to Brother Apollonius. "Stay with him. Lazar and I will seal the tomb and return home. We will return tonight under cover of deep midnight and remove you both. Pilate assures us we will not be discovered."

Apollonius agreed and added, "You better bring Matthias along with you. Dead or alive, the body will be hard to move."

Lazar and Joseph emerged from the tomb unseen by the centurion and his execution team, who were still too preoccupied with the unpleasantness of disposing of the other two corpses to notice.[14]

---

14. Editor's note: The main narrative of the Mount Carmel scrolls ends abruptly here. It is followed by the "Epilogue of Clopas." Instead of placing the epilogue here, it will appear at the end of the book.

CHAPTER SEVEN[15]

On the first day of the week, early in the morning, while it was yet
dark, Mary of Magdala came to the tomb; and she saw that the stone
was removed from the tomb. Then she ran and came to Simon Peter
and to the other disciple whom Jesus loved, and she said to them,
They have taken our Lord out of that tomb, and I do not know
where they have laid him.

—John 20:1–2

Since the crucifixion, Mary, Martha, and Jesus's mother had, for
their own safety, been secretly taken to the home of Uncle Clopas's
most trusted associates on the outskirts of Jerusalem. There they
were to wait for Jesus, Clopas, and others to join them before they
all disembarked for Smyrna and then on to Gaul. They had received
no information since they left the scene of the execution at dusk
on the Sabbath. They did not know that Jesus had been wounded
or that there had been any interruption in the Plan. Before dawn
toward the end of Sabbath night, they had still received no word.

---

15. The Toulousean scroll is the only Clopasarian document which includes this
chapter. The "Epilogue of Clopas" follows directly afterward.

"What if something has gone wrong?" Mary of Magdala kept saying. "What if he's been discovered? What if he is injured? What if they killed him? What if he is still trapped in that awful tomb?" She could no longer bear the suspense. While it was still dark, she veiled herself and set out on foot to the tomb.

Dawn was breaking by the time she reached the tomb and found the stone had been rolled from the entrance. Her heart raced as she approached the opening. Sunlight had not yet penetrated inside, and she had to wait for her eyes to adjust to the darkness. She took a few steps inside to discover the tomb empty except for a bloodied white burial cloth stretched neatly over the hewn shelf.

At first, she wanted to shout with joy. But when she picked up the blood-soaked shroud, her heart sank, and she started to panic.

"He's dead! They've killed him. They've taken his body! His horrible religious friends…or those Zealators or Caiaphas's henchmen! They have taken his body so they can somehow exploit his death!"

Her only thought was to somehow find Lazar or Brother Apollonius, but she had no idea where they might be. Most of the Galileans had scattered on the night of the arrest. She knew that Simon and the Sons of Thunder had relatives somewhere near Jerusalem, but where? She couldn't move. She just stood like a pillar of salt at the mouth of the tomb.

"Do not be afraid, sister. You will not find him here."

The voice was that of Lazar. She turned to see, but the rising sun was so bright, she did not immediately recognize him. When she finally did, she saw that he was blindingly arrayed in his Perfect Master's white robe.

"He is alive, Mary, and he wants you to go quickly and tell the Galileans. But you must say to them, 'He has risen from the dead', the same as *I* was raised from the dead. Simon, the Sons of Thunder, and the others are hiding at the home of James in Bethlehem. Go and tell them. Then return to Martha and the others. I will come soon and take you to him. Please. Go now and do as I ask."[16]

---

16. Editor's note: The main narrative of the Toulousean scrolls ends abruptly here. It is followed directly by the "Epilogue of Clopas."

EPILOGUE OF CLOPAS[17]

He came to his own, and his own did not receive him.
—*John 1:11*

It is here that I must lay the scroll down and stop reading my young friend's narrative. To my eyes, words upon the page grow faint, and my *mind's* eye cannot bear many of the scenes that I know must follow. In the scribe's mind, my memories weave an adventure, an epic story, a great tragedy, perhaps even a historical farce. For me, however, my recollections of late seem more and more like a dream—a tiny dream about a tiny people in a tiny land.

Of what importance is such a petty drama to that of the blazing of the sun or the coursing of the stars? What cosmic consequences could possibly result from my poor nephew's failure to topple a provincial regime, to become king of a little nation of myths and dreams? What consequences, indeed.

I have often heard it said, "History will prove *this*" or "History will prove *that*." But history's "proof" is the most unsubstantial and dangerous dream of all. At this very moment, the wise words of my dear nephew's ministry and the tales of his many good deeds are

---

17. The "Epilogue of Clopas" does not appear as part of the Vatican's *Confessio Clopas*, but does form the final section of the Mount Carmel, Egyptian, and Toulousean scrolls.

being twisted and distorted by monsters of political intrigue and religious fanaticism: the same evil forces that undermined the Messiah movement, the same thoughtless "disciples" who denied him, the same frightened voices that cried for his arrest and crucifixion, the same mob who brought him to the cross and who even now, with the most pernicious intentions, would proclaim him bodily ascended into the sky and worshipped as a God. Even now, a murderous former agent of Rome—a man who never met Jesus—is calling himself "apostle" and poisoning the minds of even the elect with his lies and hallucinatory gospel of fear and self-loathing.

No. History will never be able to tell my story. As much as I laud the literary efforts of my young scribe, I confess there are many secrets I have not shared with him—secrets I must reserve for the safety of + + +,[18] who now dwells near me and our family in this verdant land so far from the bloody dust of Judaea—secrets that, God willing, might preserve the vine for another season.

But I am done with plots. I have given my word, and I shall keep it. I will soon carry my secrets to the grave. James must do what he must do without the aid of his uncle Clopas. It is he who could arguably claim the mythical throne of David.

I've always been a lucky man. I was born into wealth. I married well. I traveled much. I am well educated in the arts and sciences. I have truly enjoyed the adventures of my life. My involvement in the Messiah movement has taught me that it is good to have a goal in life, but that it is *not* good to define your life by that goal. Doing so will only guarantee disappointment. All of us are accidental Christs, thrust awkwardly to stumble toward Godhood by factors infinite and unknown. If I would share my secret, I would tell you to rise from

---

18. Three crosses appear in this place in all three sets of scroll manuscripts of the "Epilogue of Clopas."

your stumbling and take wing. Welcome your accidental adventures. Enjoy the aimless winging of your soul. For in truth, our aimless winging is at once the beginning, the middle, and the end of our journey.